camp CONFIDENTIAL

Super Special!

Charmed Forces

GROSSET & DUNLAP
Published by the Penguin Group
Penguin Group (USA) Inc., 375 Hudson Street, New York,
New York 10014, USA
Penguin Group (Canada), 90 Eglinton Avenue East, Suite 700, Toronto, Ontario
M4P 2Y3, Canada (a division of Pearson Penguin Canada Inc.)
Penguin Books Ltd., 80 Strand, London WC2R 0RL, England
Penguin Group Ireland, 25 St. Stephen's Green, Dublin 2, Ireland
(a division of Penguin Books Ltd.)
Penguin Group (Australia), 250 Camberwell Road, Camberwell, Victoria 3124,
Australia (a division of Pearson Australia Group Pty. Ltd.)
Penguin Books India Pvt. Ltd., 11 Community Centre, Panchsheel Park,
New Delhi—110 017, India
Penguin Group (NZ), 67 Apollo Drive, Rosedale, North Shore 0632,
New Zealand (a division of Pearson New Zealand Ltd.)
Penguin Books (South Africa) (Pty.) Ltd., 24 Sturdee Avenue,
Rosebank, Johannesburg 2196, South Africa

Penguin Books Ltd., Registered Offices: 80 Strand, London WC2R 0RL, England

Cover design by Ching N. Chan
Front cover images © Eri Morita/Photodisc/Getty Images and
© John Arne Birkeland/iStockphoto Inc./iStock International Inc.

Library of Congress Cataloging-in-Publication Data is available.

ISBN 978-0-448-44722-3   10 9 8 7 6 5 4 3 2 1

camp CONFIDENTIAL
Super Special!

Charmed Forces

by Melissa J. Morgan

Grosset & Dunlap

chapter
ONE

Posted by: Alyssa
Subject: Camp Preview—Sixth Division Rocks!

Hello all sixth div. Lakeview chickadees! School's out and it's time for camp. Just want to let you know that I have done my research and I have a STRONG feeling this is going to be the best summer ever! All signs point to yes! (Well, *almost* all signs. With the exception of one giant one—the fact that Grace isn't coming back. I still haven't gotten used to the idea. Maybe because the news came about on such short notice. But I guess it's for the best—the more courses she takes over the summer, the more time she'll have for drama next year. Grace—you're sure going to be missed!)

In case you're wondering how I know this summer's going to be great, well, I had my first ever tarot card reading yesterday, and Lady Gisela told me that camp is going to kick it this year. She also told me I'm seriously psychic! So I bought a book about new age phenomena and am busy gathering tools to help "bring my gift to the surface," as Lady Gisela says.

Turns out a psychic needs a lot of stuff, like crystals, tarot cards, astrology books, herbs . . . I'm just getting started.

Here's what I know so far about the next two months:

Horoscope: "As Jupiter moves into Cancer and squares with Mercury, this summer is all about magic! Friendship, love, and nature play strong roles." Friendship, love, and nature? Sounds just like camp!

Ouija board: A friend of mine from school, Tally, slept over last night and we did the Ouija board. We asked the spirits what kind of summer we'll have. The spirits told Tally that she'll be fighting off a cold for most of July, but they told *me* that this summer will be full of sun and fun. Poor Tally—but yay us!

The I Ching:
Li/The Clinging, Fire
The Judgment: The Clinging.
Perseverance brings success.
Care of the cow brings good fortune.

Can't argue with that, can you? Maybe there will be a cow at camp we can take care of. Or something. Okay, I don't really know which cow the I Ching is talking about, but whatever, trust me, it's good.

So buckle your seat belts—it's going to be one for the record books! Can't wait to see you all on Sunday! And Grace—this one's for you!

Love, Alyssa

you're psychic now? i guess that fits with the rest of your personality, your royal artsiness. but you forgot one great fortune-telling source—what did the magic 8-ball say?

xo, nat

Hate to break it to you, Nat, but everyone knows the Magic 8-Ball doesn't really tell fortunes. It's a toy. But since I'm thorough, I checked it anyway. I asked, "Will this be the best summer ever for the sixth division at Camp Lakeview?" Answer: "Reply hazy, try again." I tried again. This time the answer was: "Cannot predict now."

Which only proves my point: The Magic 8-Ball doesn't work.

▲ ▲ ▲

"Just as I predicted," Alyssa said. "This summer is starting off right."

She stepped off the bus from New Jersey onto sacred soil—Camp Lakeview soil. The campgrounds looked even better than last year, with fresh paint on the bunks and the lodge and the mess hall, the dirt paths newly swept and repaired, and even a sparkling new CAMP LAKEVIEW sign at the entrance.

Alyssa took another step and lost her footing.

A small, round rock had rolled under her foot and nearly tripped her. She bent down in front of the bus door and picked it up. Chelsea, who was getting off the bus behind Alyssa, bumped into her.

"Ohh!" Chelsea said. "Sorry, Alyssa." She wound her long blond hair into a knot on top of her head and popped her gum.

"Look at this." Alyssa showed Chelsea a rock the size of a walnut, rough and mostly grayish-brown, with a few glints of deep purple shining through.

Could it be an amethyst? Alyssa wondered. She had been looking for one. She'd read that amethysts promoted healing and psychic awareness, especially when touching the skin. They also helped people interpret dreams. They were practically magic! Every psychic should have one.

"So?" Chelsea said. "It's a rock. This place is crawling with them." She moved Alyssa aside so Natalie, Gaby, and Valerie could get off the bus. They all gathered around to see what Alyssa had found.

"It's not very pretty," Gaby said. "Except for that purplish part."

"I think it's an amethyst, and amethysts are very lucky," Alyssa said. "I'm going to go to the nature shack and find out."

"I'm going to go to the kitchen and lock myself in the walk-in freezer," Chelsea said. "It's so hot!"

"Tell me about it." Gaby wiped the sweat off her forehead. "It's only June. I thought the mountains were supposed to be *cool*."

"Maybe it will cool off tonight." Alyssa tossed her long black braid over her shoulder and hoisted her duffel bag. The girls started down the familiar path to their bunk, 6B. Their division was still small, like last year, so all the sixth-division girls would share one cabin.

The weather was unusually hot for the Poconos, but Alyssa didn't like to complain. She was fourteen now; this would be her last summer as a camper at Camp Lakeview and she was determined to enjoy it. Her parents had hinted that next year she might have to get a summer job.

As part of the camp's new look, each freshly painted bunk had a different color door: red, yellow, green, blue, orange, pink, turquoise . . .

"Look at the bunks!" Valerie said. "The doors have been painted new colors."

"I wonder what color door our bunk will have?" Natalie said.

"Care to make a prediction, O Mighty Alyssa?" Gaby said.

Before they reached bunk 6B, Alyssa guessed, "Our door will be purple. In honor of the good-luck rock I just found."

She and Chelsea rounded the corner in the path at the same moment. Alyssa gasped. Natalie, Valerie, and Gaby gasped, too.

"Oh my gosh," Natalie said. "Alyssa, you were right!"

There, nestled among the trees, stood their brown wooden cabin. The bright purple door had a white 6B painted on it.

Alyssa rubbed the stone between her fingers. "Huh," she said. "I had a feeling about this thing."

"That was just a lucky guess," Chelsea said.

"Pretty lucky," Valerie said. "I never would have guessed purple."

The girls stepped inside their cabin. Alyssa dumped her duffel on a top bunk near the window. Natalie took the bunk below hers. And then, as if on cue, they both noticed a tall, glamorous blond girl sitting quietly on her bunk, painting her toenails fuchsia.

"Tori!" Alyssa said.

Tori jumped to her feet. "You're here!" She hugged Alyssa and all the other girls, one by one.

"Where is everybody?" Alyssa asked.

Tori leaned back on her bunk bed, propping her feet on the wall and wiggling her bright pink toes. "They were complaining about the heat, so Mandy took them down to the lake for a dip. They'll be back soon."

"Mandy's our new counselor?" Valerie asked.

"Uh-huh," Tori said. "She's nice, but she's not the kind of girl who understands the need for fresh pink toenail polish when you first get to camp—know what I mean? I had to do some talking to convince her to let me stay here and wait for you guys."

"We're glad you did," Gaby said as she began unpacking.

"It's so great to see you!" Natalie said.

"It's so great to see everybody!" Alyssa said. "But I have a little errand to do. I'll be back in a few minutes." She hurried off to the nature shack, clutching the rough stone. Why did she feel so attached to it already? So excited about it? Something about those glints of purple . . .

The nature shack was quiet and deserted. Alyssa went to the library shelf and grabbed a book called *The Geologist's Handbook*. She paged through it until she came to a picture of a rock that looked a lot like the one she'd found. There were two photos, sort of like before and after shots. The first picture showed a rough, grayish-brown rock with a slight grape tinge, like the one she held in her hand.

The other photo made her gasp.

It showed a glorious, gleaming cut and polished purple gem. An amethyst.

"I was right," Alyssa said to herself. The rock she'd found was an uncut, unpolished amethyst. Just what she needed to enhance her psychic powers.

Alyssa rubbed the amethyst happily. She was sure now that her predictions were right. This summer was going to be magical.

▲ ▲ ▲

Alyssa practically skipped back to bunk 6B, squeezing her way through the hordes of arriving campers lugging bags and boxes. She burst through the purple door. The cabin was crowded with girls now. Chelsea was taping up a Justin Timberlake poster and everyone else was oohing and aahing over some photos Natalie was passing around.

"Alyssa, look!" Natalie said. "My new puppy!" She showed Alyssa a photo of an adorable little boxer. "A gift from Dad. I named him Tumtum."

"A boxer! Way to go, Tad," Alyssa said. Natalie's father, Tad Maxwell, was a movie star. Nat spent most of the year with her mother, so Tad tried to make up for his absence with presents—and they were usually awesome. "That is the cutest puppy I've ever seen."

"Alyssa, hi. You're my last camper unaccounted for." A freckle-faced, athletic girl in shorts and sneakers gave Alyssa's hand a firm shake. Then she made a checkmark on her clipboard. She wore her chestnut hair in a practical ponytail. "I'm Mandy, your counselor. Welcome!"

"Thanks," Alyssa said. "Hi, everybody."

"Alyssa!" Dramatic Brynn bounded off her bunk to give Alyssa a hug. Next in line were mischievous Jenna, jock Alex, tomboy Priya, and shy Candace. Not that the girls' complex personalities could be summed up in one word or anything.

"It's so great to see you all!" Alyssa cried, and she meant it. It was wonderful to see her friends all in one bunk again. They'd have the whole summer together.

Alyssa noticed an unfamiliar face among her friends and stepped forward to introduce herself. "Are you new? I'm Alyssa."

"I'm Sloan," the girl said. She had curly auburn hair, deep brown eyes, and a round, thoughtful face. Alyssa liked her right away. "I am new. But you're all so friendly, I already feel like I belong. Kind of."

Alyssa smiled. "You'll fit in fine. It won't take long."

"When you share a cabin with twelve people, you get to know them pretty fast," Jenna said.

"Hey, Liss—what did you find out about your lucky rock?" Natalie asked.

"I was right," Alyssa said. "It's a real amethyst."

Everyone crowded around to look at it, even

Chelsea and Gaby, who'd dissed the rock earlier.

"May I see it?" Sloan took the amethyst and held it up to the light from the window. "Yes," she said, nodding. "This is a powerful one."

"Do you know a lot about rocks, Sloan?" Mandy asked.

"Not rocks in general," Sloan said. "But I do know about crystals and psychic phenomena, and amethysts can play an important part. My mother is a past life regression therapist."

Alyssa couldn't help noticing as Chelsea and Alex exchanged a skeptical look.

"Really? Wow," Alyssa said. She'd always wanted to have her past lives analyzed.

"What in the world is that?" Gaby asked.

"It's kind of like a psychotherapist, but with a different method," Sloan explained. "If you're having a problem in your life, some obstacle you can't get past, you go to my mother and she hypnotizes you."

"That doesn't sound very scientific," Chelsea said. "How do you know it works?"

"She's changed people's lives," Sloan said. "She hypnotizes you so you can relive your past lives and find out where the problem is. If you can solve the problem in your past life, it goes away in your present life."

"Oh, that *proves* it works," Chelsea snapped.

"Chelsea," Mandy said. "Let's all be respectful."

"Yeah," Valerie said. "What happened to trying to be nice, Chelsea?"

Chelsea had once been a meanie, but was trying to improve herself. She ducked her head and said, "Right—I keep forgetting. I meant to say, sounds interesting. Tell me more." She mustered a smile. Alyssa thought it didn't look entirely sincere, but it was a good effort.

"Past life regression is not that weird," Priya said. "A lot of people believe in reincarnation."

"Especially where I come from," Sloan said.

"Where do you come from?" Valerie asked.

"Sedona, Arizona," Sloan said. "Psychic Headquarters of the U.S.A. We've got crystals, clairvoyants, gurus, and more UFO sightings per capita than anyplace else in the country, except maybe Roswell."

I knew I liked this girl, Alyssa thought.

"Better finish unpacking, girls," Mandy said. "The cookout starts in an hour."

"Cookout." Sloan made a face. "It's way too hot to eat heavy, greasy meat."

Every summer the camp held a welcome cookout on the first evening. They served hamburgers, hot dogs, potato salad, the usual. It was a Lakeview tradition.

"I usually have potato salad and watermelon," Alyssa said. She was a vegetarian. "It's not my favorite meal."

"Maybe this year they'll serve something lighter for a change," Natalie said. "Because of the heat wave."

"That would be awesome," Alyssa said. She opened her duffel bag and pulled out a pile of T-shirts. "Something light like salad. Or even pasta. It's too hot for hot dogs."

"I like the cookout," Valerie said. "It's fun to see everyone again."

"Yeah," Gaby said. "Who cares what they're serving? It's a chance to check out the cute new boys."

Tori shrugged. "Things are great with Michael. I'm off the market." Michael was her boyfriend in L.A.

"David and I planned to meet up at the cookout," Jenna said. "I haven't seen him in ages."

"And I can't wait to see Adam again," Alex said.

Jenna laughed. "Don't worry, he hasn't changed a bit—unfortunately." Alex's boyfriend, Adam, also happened to be Jenna's twin brother.

"What about you, Brynn?" Alyssa asked. "Are you and Jordan going to get back together?"

"I don't know yet," Brynn said. "We left things kind of up in the air." She twisted her hair nervously. "It's kind of hard, not knowing. Has he said anything about it to you, Priya?"

Priya shook her head. Brynn's ex-boyfriend, Jordan, was Priya's best friend. "We don't talk about that stuff anymore. I think he's afraid I'll leak his secrets to you."

"Of course you would," Brynn said. "That's what bunkmates are for!"

Priya just shrugged. "All we talk about lately is soccer, baseball, and food. Which is cool, I guess. If I liked a good friend of his, I'm not sure how much I'd want to tell him, either."

"I guess I'll find out how he's feeling tonight," Brynn said.

"I'm in the same boat with Logan," Natalie said. "We only broke up because the long-distance thing was getting too hard. Our plan was to see how we felt once we got back to camp, but now I feel really awkward around him. Especially since I met Reed in L.A. Uggghhhh! I'm all confused!" Natalie had met Reed, the son of a famous director, while visiting her dad in Los Angeles. But since Nat lived in New York, things never had a chance to get serious.

"Are you and Reed official?" Alyssa asked.

"Not really," Natalie said. "We promised to keep in touch. We didn't say anything about being official boyfriend/girlfriend, or about not seeing other people."

"So that means you're free," Valerie said. "Like me."

"And me," Priya said.

"And me," Chelsea said. "For a change of pace . . ." Chelsea was very pretty, but she'd never had a boyfriend at camp. Maybe because she knew all too well how pretty she was. And also because she used to be, well, *difficult* was the nice way of putting it, Alyssa thought.

"And me," Sloan said. "The only boy I know here is my brother, Alaric."

"Is he cute?" Gaby said.

"Adorable," Sloan said. "But he's only ten. What about the counselors? Are they mascara-worthy, or is it a waste of energy?"

"There are a few cute new ones every year," Gaby said.

"Well, I'm staying off boys this year," Candace

said. "I've declared this to be a boy-free summer."

"What?" said Brynn. "Why?"

"Why? Boys are too distracting," Candace said. "Next year we'll be in ninth grade, and it'll be time to start applying to high schools. I've got to save my energy for my schoolwork—and my extracurriculars."

"That sounds to me like your parents talking," Brynn said.

"It does sound like my parents talking . . ." Candace said. She had an awkward tendency to repeat what other people said. She was known as the Human Echo. "Well, they were the ones who got me thinking. They said they thought it would be smart to keep away from boys for the summer. I'm going to concentrate on sailing. It's the one sport I have a chance at a scholarship in. It's not nearly as popular as basketball and soccer."

"We'll see if you stick to that," Valerie said.

"I'll stick to it. I've got to try, at least," Candace said. "I promised my parents."

Alyssa had never seen Candace talk so much. She must have been more comfortable around everyone now that she and Brynn were friends at school.

"What about you, Alyssa?" Natalie asked.

Alyssa shrugged. "I'm going to wait and see. If it happens, it happens. If it doesn't, it wasn't meant to be."

"You are getting way too mellow," Gaby said.

Chelsea collapsed on her bed and fanned herself with a magazine. "Ugh, it's almost too hot to think about boys. Why isn't this stupid camp air-conditioned?"

"I don't care how hot it gets," Gaby said. "Bring on the boys!"

"I'm skipping dinner," Candace said, "and going right for the watermelon."

"Check out the guy *slicing* the watermelon," Priya said. "New counselor?"

When it was time for dinner, Candace and the rest of bunk 6B trooped over to the big soccer field for the cookout. The field was already crowded with campers old and new and the food lines were long.

A blond, tan, surfer-type in a counselor's green T-shirt was cutting watermelon slices for the dessert buffet. Candace hadn't noticed him at first, but now that Priya mentioned it, he *was* extremely cute. She immediately tried to shove that thought from her mind. But her friends were no help.

Tori growled like a cat at the sight of the new counselor. "I think I'll start with some watermelon, too."

"Remember, you're off the market, Tori," Valerie said.

"I know," Tori said. "And I'm glad. But sometimes, you know—it's a shame."

The girls went to the watermelon station to grab slices to tide them over while they stood in the dinner line.

"Hi," Tori said to the cute new counselor.

"Hi," he said. He sliced open another melon while Tori took a plate.

"Hi," Valerie said, taking her piece.

"Hi." The counselor glanced up at them and smiled, but he was too busy to flirt. "Keep the line moving, girls."

Candace grabbed her slice and followed the others to the grill line, which snaked around the picnic tables. Looking at the sea of faces, she felt happy to be back. The little first-year kids ran around shrieking with excitement, chased by their harried counselors. The older kids sat back, checking one another out, or ran squealing across the field to hug old friends.

Meanwhile, Candace's friends—the senior girls of the camp—scoped the boys. And they weren't the only ones.

"What's going on over by the drink station?" Jenna asked.

A swarm of girls buzzed like flies around a picnic table loaded with ice and sodas. Surely they couldn't all be that thirsty.

The crowd of girls parted for a brief second and Candace caught a glimpse of the boy at its center. Tall, tan, a mop of wavy dark hair, a puka shell around his neck on a leather strap, a Puma T-shirt, and best of all, a wide, easy smile.

"Nothing wrong with *that*," Valerie said.

"Nothing at all," Chelsea added, munching her watermelon.

"Dibs!" Gaby said. "He's mine."

"You can't call dibs on a boy," Valerie said. The line moved and they all took a few steps forward.

"I think I just did," Gaby said.

"I think it's a *little* more complicated than that," Valerie said. "Doesn't the boy get any say in the matter?"

"Not if I have anything to do with it," Gaby

said, all glitter eye shadow and determination. She beelined for the guy. Priya and Valerie trailed after her, forfeiting their places in line.

"Hey!" Chelsea called as she ran after them. "You can't get away with this!"

Candace licked watermelon juice off her fingers and moved forward in the line, which had just gotten a little shorter.

"Is everybody at this camp always so boy crazy?" Sloan asked.

"Boy crazy? This year looks like it's going to be worse than usual," Candace said.

"That guy *is* pretty cute," Alyssa said.

"You think?" Candace stood on a picnic bench to get a better look at him. "Yeah, I guess he is. Everybody else sure thinks so."

"I wonder who will snag him," Alyssa said.

"If anyone does," Sloan said. She finished her melon and tossed the rind in a garbage can.

"Do you think he'll ask someone to the Midsummer Dance?" Brynn said.

"I don't think he'll have a choice," Alyssa said.

"Want to take bets?" Jenna said. "I think Chelsea's going to snag him."

"I think he'll go for Valerie," Brynn said. "If he's got any taste at all."

"Hey—the line's moving on without us," Candace said. She pressed on Alyssa's back to move the group forward.

"Maybe he'll end up with a fifth-division girl," Alyssa said.

"Boo. Hiss," Brynn said. "That's no fun." She spit

a watermelon seed onto her plate.

"Poor guy," Candace said. "We don't even know what his name is yet and we're already making matches for him."

"Poor guy? Please," Sloan said. "I don't see him suffering much, do you?"

The crowd parted and the guy carried his soda to a picnic table full of sixth-division guys. The girls tagged after him, offering more soda, a napkin, a plate.

"Look at them," Brynn said.

"Look at them. Pathetic," Candace said. "One thing I promise you: That is *not* going to be me this summer."

"Let's get something to eat," Alyssa said.

The girls finally reached the head of the line. They picked up paper plates and napkins and plastic forks and spoons. Mandy ran over to join them. "Here you are!" she said. "May I cut in?"

Candace made room for her. "I'm starving," she said. "But I really don't feel like a hamburger or a hot dog."

Two counselors manned the grills. Just beyond them was a table laden with ketchup, mustard, relish, buns, and . . . pasta salad.

"Oh my gosh," Brynn said.

"Alyssa, look! They've got pasta salad!" Candace said. "Just like you predicted!"

Alyssa's jaw dropped. "Wow. That's . . . amazing."

"Oh, come on," Mandy said. "It's a hot night. It makes sense that they'd serve something lighter than usual. They must have served pasta salad before—haven't they?"

"I don't remember ever having it at the welcome cookout," Jenna said. "And I've been coming here forever."

"Maybe it was before your time," Mandy said.

"Alyssa," Brynn said, "the amethyst was right!"

"Maybe it really does have powers," Alyssa said.

"Of course it does," Sloan said. "That's what amethysts do. They heighten your psychic powers."

"Come on, girls," Mandy said. "Let's not blow this out of proportion. It's a coincidence."

Candace looked at Alyssa, who skipped the grill and loaded up her plate with pasta salad. "You really didn't know ahead of time?" Candace asked her.

"I really didn't," Alyssa said. "I swear. I'm as blown away by this as you are."

chapter TWO

As soon as Gaby saw the adorable boy in the puka shell necklace, she forgot about food. The cookout became all about him. The enticing smells of grilling meat, the sound of gossip, the heat of the day . . . all that fell away and she focused on the adorable boy.

The adorable boy walked from his picnic table to the food line to the watermelon table and back to the drinks table, trailed by girls wherever he went. Gaby couldn't get him alone. She knew she'd make no impression on him as long as he was surrounded by the competition. And the competition included several of her bunkmates.

"Give it up, Gaby," Chelsea said. "We'll have other chances to meet the guy."

Aha. The competition was starting to fade. "Heading for the food tables?" Gaby said.

"I'm hungry," Chelsea said. "We've been here for an hour and we haven't eaten yet. All we've done is follow this guy around."

"Hunger is for the weak," Gaby said. "You

go ahead and give up. I want to at least find out his name."

"He's cute, but he's no Justin Timberlake," Chelsea said. "Want me to bring you a burger?"

Gaby waved her away. "I'm beyond food."

At last, like magic, the swarm of girls disappeared. It was as if someone had sprayed some kind of anti-girl pesticide into the crowd. *They've given up*, Gaby thought. *Wimps. But I have the stamina to outlast any girl with a mere crush. This is beyond a crush. This is . . . fate.* Not to get all Alyssa about it.

"Hi," Gaby said, sidling up to the boy.

"Hi." The boy looked startled to see her. Gaby was surprised. He should have been used to girls introducing themselves to him by now.

They were standing at the end of a long line. Gaby didn't care what they were waiting for. She assumed it was ice cream or something. The line moved slightly. The boy stepped forward. Gaby stepped forward, too.

"First year at Lakeview?" Gaby asked.

"Yep," the guy said. "I used to go to a sailing camp on the Chesapeake, but it closed down last year."

"We've got sailing here," Gaby said. She wasn't much of a sailor herself, but she made a mental note to sign up for sailing immediately.

"I know," the guy said. The line moved again, and the guy took another step forward. "That's why I came here. Plus I thought it would be fun to do some other activities besides sailing, for a change of pace."

"Gotcha," Gaby said. "Jewelry-making is fun. So's ceramics."

"Uh, yeah," the boy said. "I was thinking more along the lines of baseball, soccer, maybe photography."

"Those are all great, too," Gaby said. So, he was a jock. Sports weren't really Gaby's thing, but how hard could photography be? Point, snap, you're done. That could work . . .

The line moved forward a few steps. Another guy got in line behind them.

"So, I'm Gaby, by the way," Gaby said to the adorable boy.

"Donovan," the boy said.

Donovan. Yes! A total hottie name. "If you need anyone to show you around or if you have any questions or anything, you can totally ask me," Gaby said. "I've been going here since I was ten, which is, you know, a long time."

"Awesome," Donovan said. "Thanks, Gaby." The line moved forward again. "Actually, I do have a question for you."

"Ooh, what's that?" Gaby beamed, ready to help with whatever totally hot problems Donovan might have.

"Why are you standing in line for the boys' bathroom?"

Gaby looked around. It was true: The line she stood in was made up entirely of boys. Why hadn't she noticed that before? And it ended at the boys' bathroom. No wonder she'd finally been able to get Donovan alone!

The other boys in line laughed. Gaby's face got hot. She looked like an idiot, and she felt like one, too.

But in true Gaby form, she tried to cover her mistake with bravado.

"I just thought you might like some company while you waited," she said. "But I guess I'd better get out of here before I find myself standing in front of a urinal."

The boys laughed again, and Gaby hurried away. *Rats,* she thought. So much for getting off on the right foot. She'd really stepped in it this time.

Well, at least she'd made an impression on him. Out of all the girls he'd met that day, he wouldn't forget the one who stood in line for the boys' bathroom, that was for sure. She'd have time to make a better impression later. Like maybe at sailing practice . . .

⛺ ⛺ ⛺

"There's Jordan." Brynn gripped Alex's arm, her heart suddenly beating faster.

"He looks good," Alex said, and Brynn agreed. His messy brown hair was even longer than it had been a few months ago, and his green eyes seemed, impossibly, greener than ever. He batted a beach ball around with a thin girl whose dark hair was plaited into a thick, heavy braid.

"Who's that girl with him?" Brynn asked Alex.

"I'm not sure," Alex said. "I think she's in fifth division."

Jordan spotted them. He smiled and waved, but he didn't come over to say hello. The dark-haired girl turned around to see who he was waving to. Then he hit the beach ball to her and she swatted it back.

"That's it?" Brynn said. "A little wave, and back

to the game?" She wanted to turn away, to stop watching him, but she couldn't. He shook his hair and her heartbeat sped up even more.

"It does seem a little strange," Alex said. "But he's busy. Maybe he'll say hello later."

"Later?" Later didn't seem good enough. Brynn was surprised at the force of her reaction. She hadn't seen Jordan in a few months, and she'd been curious to see how he'd changed, how she'd feel about him. They hadn't been sure if they'd get back together this summer, and that had been fine. They'd decided to play it by ear, see how they felt, blah blah blah, and she was cool with that.

But she hadn't expected this. To feel so emotional at the sight of him. One look and *bam!*—she was right back where they left off. Crazy for him.

"You could go over and say hi, too, you know," Alex said.

"I know," Brynn said. "But I want him to come to me."

If only she knew how he felt, everything would be easier. But this wondering . . . it was hard. Did he like that girl he was playing with, whoever she was? Hadn't he missed Brynn at all since they broke up?

"Come on—let's go get you some cookies." Alex pulled her away toward the dessert table, where Jenna and her twin brother, Adam, were munching on snickerdoodles. Alex didn't have these problems. She and Adam were as tight as Brynn's waistband after Make Your Own Sundae night.

"I can't take this," Brynn moaned. "If Jordan's going to be weird and noncommittal all summer, I'll lose my mind. I'll have to leave Lakeview and check myself into a psychiatric hospital that deals with love-lorn trauma—"

"Stop being so dramatic," Alex said, but Brynn couldn't help it. Being dramatic was her nature. "He smiled, didn't he? He waved. He's not avoiding you. It will all work out."

"I hope you're right," Brynn said. "Because if you're wrong, it's going to be a long hot summer."

"I hope it's a long hot summer anyway," Alex said calmly.

Brynn sighed. Alex didn't understand. She was always so levelheaded. How did she do it?

▲　▲　▲

"Hey, Nat. What's up?" Logan stopped Natalie on her way to the salad table. He was manning the bar-becue, cooking hamburgers and hot dogs in an apron that said BOY MEETS GRILL, with a cartoon picture of a grill with eyes, lips, and legs in high heels.

"Not much," Natalie said. Logan was more gor-geous than ever. Even a cheesy apron couldn't make him look bad.

"Are you okay?" he asked. "You look a little . . . I don't know . . . worried or something."

Actually, Natalie *was* worried about something. Just before she'd left for camp, the vet had found a lump on her boxer Tumtum's abdomen. They were going to do tests this week to make sure the lump wasn't cancer. Her mother had promised to take good care of the puppy no matter what. Still, Natalie couldn't help being worried about him. But she hadn't told anyone about the tumor. It could turn out to be benign, so why upset everyone over nothing?

And now, instead of burdening Logan with her troubles, she only said, "No, everything's fine. I'm just hot, that's all."

Logan wiped a sweaty lock of blond hair out of his eyes. "Please—I'm boiling back here. Can I interest you in a greaseburger?"

Natalie laughed. "I'm going for the pasta salad, so no thanks."

"Didn't think so. I'd offer you sushi if I had any. You still like sushi, don't you?"

"Totally," Natalie said.

"That's good," Logan said. "I'm glad to know some things never change."

A pale ten-year-old boy with straight black hair in a bowl cut tugged on Logan's shirt. "Logan, can I have another hot dog?"

"How many have you had, buddy?" Logan asked. He was a CIT this year. Natalie figured this boy was in his bunk.

"Four," the boy said.

"I think that's enough for now," Logan said. "Save some room for s'mores."

"I was going to make a s'more hot dog," the boy said.

Natalie made a face. "A s'more hot dog? What's that?"

"You put a hot dog, a marshmallow, and some chocolate between two graham crackers. Then you force-feed it to one of the first-division kids," the boy said.

"Sweet," Natalie said.

"Now I'm definitely not giving you a hot dog," Logan said.

"Party pooper." The boy walked off, muttering, "I'll just have to feed them ants instead."

"Nice kid," Natalie joked.

Logan shook his head. "They're devils. You have no idea what boys can get up to."

"Were you like that when you were little?" Natalie asked.

"I guess I must have been, but I don't remember force-feeding ants to anybody," Logan said. "I must have blocked out the memory."

Nat smiled, but she didn't know what to say next. She had run out of conversation topics. Tumtum was on her mind, but she didn't want to bring that up—too depressing—and Logan wasn't helping. He made himself busy poking the coals and turning the hot dogs with his tongs.

I wonder if he's going to want to get back together this summer? she thought. She was still in touch with Reed, the very sweet boy she'd met visiting her dad in L.A. And she still thought about Reed a lot. But now here was Logan, standing right in front of her, looking supercute . . . and she and Logan would be together at camp all summer, while Reed was all the way across the country . . . Still, cute and charming as Logan was, he could be full of himself sometimes. Nat was torn. She wondered again what he was thinking, if he wanted to get back together. And then she wondered, *Do I?*

The silence lasted uncomfortably long. "Well,"

Natalie began. "I guess I'll go get some pasta salad."

"Okay," Logan said. "See you later, maybe?"

A little girl came up behind Natalie and held out a plate with a hot dog bun on it. "Can I please have a hot dog?" she asked Logan.

"Sure." Logan took her plate and put a fresh hot dog on her bun. "There you go."

The little girl picked up the hot dog and took a bite. "Ow! My tongue! I burnt my tongue!" She dropped her plate in the dirt, hot dog and all, and started crying.

"Are you okay?" Nat asked, but the girl wouldn't stop screeching.

"That hot dog was too hot!" the girl said.

Logan came out from behind the grill. "I'm so sorry! Let's go get some ice for your tongue." He took the little girl's hand. "I'd better take care of this, Nat. See you."

"See you." Logan led the girl to the drink table. Nat moved on to get some pasta salad. So much for easy answers. So far the whole Logan situation was inconclusive at best.

chapter

THREE

"Good morning, sleepyhead." Alyssa's upside-down face floated, smiling, over Natalie. Natalie sat up and rubbed her eyes. She'd been dreaming. What was Alyssa doing in her bedroom?

"Yoo-hoo, earth to Natalie," Alyssa said. She climbed down from her bunk and sat on Natalie's bed, clutching her amethyst in one hand. "Rough night?"

Natalie's head began to clear. *Oh, right,* she thought. *I'm at camp.* Sunlight poured into the cabin. She was happy to see all her bunkmates around her, waking up for the first full day at Lakeview.

"I had such a weird dream," Natalie said. "I was back in New York, but I couldn't get into my apartment. I'd lost my key. I kept looking for it, all along the sidewalk and through the hallway of my building . . ."

Valerie got up and started getting dressed. "That's awful. I hate those dreams when you can't find something."

"At least now you know it isn't real," Priya said. "It was just a dream."

"I wonder why I dreamed that, though?" Natalie said. "I wish I knew what it meant."

"Maybe Alyssa can tell you," Sloan said. "Amethysts are supposed to help interpret dreams."

"That's right," Alyssa said. "Let me think about this a minute." She closed her eyes and rubbed the amethyst between her hands. She squinted as if thinking hard, but after a few seconds her face relaxed into a frown of concentration.

"I'm getting a feeling," she said. "You lost something . . . your key. The key to your house. You—you're worried. You're worried about something you care about, something that's out of your reach. Or maybe a person. Someone you left behind at home." She opened her eyes and blinked at Natalie. "Does that sound right?"

"I don't believe it," Natalie said. She hadn't meant to share her worry with the whole bunk, but this was too eerie to keep secret. "You're right, Alyssa. I *am* worried about someone at home. My puppy, Tumtum."

"Wow. This thing is incredible." Alyssa stared at the amethyst as if she almost didn't believe it herself.

"Your puppy, Tumtum—is something wrong with him?" Candace asked.

"He has a tumor," Natalie confessed. "Or at least, a suspicious lump in his belly."

"Oh, no!" the whole bunk gathered around in sympathy. "Is he going to be okay?"

"I don't know yet," Nat said. "The vet did a biopsy to see if it's cancer or not. They're supposed to call my Mom with the results today."

"That's terrible," Alex said.

"I'm so sorry, Natalie," Mandy said. "I hope he'll be all right."

"I didn't want to say anything until I heard the results." Natalie stared at Alyssa, who gripped her stone. "But—you saw it! How did you know?"

Alyssa shrugged. "I don't know. It just came to me."

"Just like the words *pasta* and *salad* came to you yesterday," Sloan said. "And then we went to the cookout and they had pasta salad."

"Yeah," Tori said. "That is weird."

"What about the biopsy?" Natalie asked Alyssa. "Can you tell if Tumtum will be okay?"

"I don't know," Alyssa said.

"Try it," Valerie said.

"Okay." Alyssa closed her eyes again and rubbed the stone. "I'm concentrating on Tumtum . . ."

The cabin was silent while she squeezed the amethyst. All the girls froze in place, watching Alyssa and holding their breath, Natalie most of all. At last Alyssa opened her eyes.

"Well?"

"I predict that the tumor will be benign," Alyssa said. "Tumtum will be okay."

A collective sigh of relief filled the room as the girls relaxed. One by one they began to change out of their pajamas and into their shorts and T-shirts.

"Oh, I hope you're right," Natalie said. She and Alyssa were the only two who hadn't started dressing yet.

"We'll see," Chelsea said. She reached under

her bunk, searching for a missing sock. "When will you find out, Natalie?"

"I'm supposed to call my mother this afternoon," Natalie said. "I'll let you all know what she says." She went to her cubby and started pulling out her clothes for the day.

"All right, girls," Mandy said. "That's enough psychic hotline for this morning. Time to pick your electives. I'll write down your first three choices while you're getting dressed. Then, after breakfast, I'll work out the schedules while you're taking your swim tests. Natalie, I'll start with you."

"I'll take drama, photography, and ceramics," Natalie said, pulling a blue cotton top over her head.

Mandy wrote this down on her clipboard. "Good. Okay, next. Alyssa?"

Alyssa rubbed the amethyst, thinking. "Give me . . . nature and arts and crafts. For a backup, I'll take photography."

Natalie put on her shorts and sneakers while Mandy finished writing down everyone's preferences.

"Oh, and there's a special event this afternoon, right after lunch," Mandy announced. "An obstacle course, with prizes for individual campers and for the winning bunks. We'll be competing against bunk 5C."

"Great!" Alyssa said. Natalie watched her give the stone another rub before hiding it away in the toe of her extra pair of sneakers. "I hope we win!"

"Mandy, is it okay if I skip the obstacle course?" Natalie asked. "I need to call home this afternoon . . ."

Mandy's no-nonsense face softened. "Right,

about Tumtum. Sure, Natalie. You're excused from the obstacle course."

"Thanks, Mandy," Natalie said. "I'm not much good at that stuff, anyway. I'll let you all know what my mother says as soon as I talk to her."

"I hope he's okay," Valerie said.

Alyssa put her hand on Natalie's shoulder. "He will be. I can feel it."

"I hope you're right," Natalie said.

⛺ ⛺ ⛺

"Is there a new cook?" Alyssa said as they trooped from the mess hall to the lake after breakfast. "That French toast was actually tasty."

"I saw someone new in the kitchen. I guess Pete didn't come back this summer. I'll miss him and all, but I won't miss his burned French toast," Jenna said.

"And they served it with fruit salad," Tori added. "Nice touch."

Alyssa's morning was going well. A good breakfast for a change, and a beautiful blue-sky day. Next up: Swim test.

Alyssa usually hated swim tests, especially in the chilly lake in the morning. But the day was so hot, she volunteered to go first, and the water felt wonderful. She passed her test with flying colors and wouldn't have to take lessons with the younger girls, as she'd feared, but with the advanced swim group like most of the others in her bunk.

She spent the rest of the test period floating on her back and staring at the puffy clouds as they drifted overhead. One by one her bunkmates joined her as they finished their tests. A dragonfly skipped over the surface of the lake. Little boys kayaked in the distance. A light breeze shook the lush green trees.

"Aah," Alyssa said. "This is what summer camp is all about."

"Totally," Sloan said.

"Yeah," Alex said. "This plus Color War."

Alex was right, Alyssa thought. This peace and quiet wouldn't last. Soon the contests would begin, rivalries would heat up, bunks would fight to prove their superiority. *Camp isn't just about dreamy sunny mornings. It's also about cutthroat competition—unfortunately,* Alyssa thought. *It's how you blend the two that makes a good summer.*

▲ ▲ ▲

Mandy was waiting for them when they got back to the cabin to change out of their wet bathing suits. "I posted your elective assignments on the door," she said.

The girls crowded around the door to look. Alyssa picked the amethyst out of her shoe and rubbed it for good luck. Then she checked the list. She had nature and arts and crafts—her first two choices. Yes!

"Great! I'm working on the newspaper," Brynn said.

"Rats, I didn't get photography," Gaby said.

"I did," Chelsea said, gloating. "And Gaby, guess who's also taking photography? Probably, I mean."

"He said he might sign up for it," Gaby said. Everybody knew who *he* was—Donovan. "That doesn't mean he'll get it. And there's always sailing."

"Sailing?" Chelsea said. "Is that what he's into?"

"Oh—you didn't know?" Gaby said gleefully. "Yes, Donovan's huge into sailing. I signed up for it for my sports elective."

"Really?" Valerie said. "So did I."

"Me too," Candace said.

"Well, I'll just sign up for sailing, too," Chelsea said. "Then I'll have *two* activities with Donovan, and you'll only have one."

"That's *if* he gets photography," Gaby said.

That's when Mandy piped in. "Chelsea, I'm pretty sure sailing is completely filled up. Sorry."

Chelsea looked like she might pop a vein.

"Girls, girls, chill," Sloan said. "If the fates want to throw you together with Donovan, they will. If they don't, they won't. You can't fight the universe."

"The fates? Fight the universe?" Gaby said. "What are you talking about?"

"Sloan's right," Alyssa said. "Go with the flow."

"You're only saying that now because you got your first choice electives," Gaby said to Alyssa.

"You've got to become one with nature," Alyssa said. "Especially nature's rock formations." She pulled the amethyst out of her extra sneaker, kissed it, and then stuffed it back in. "I'm off to arts and crafts. I think I'll make an amethyst holder."

▲ ▲ ▲

"Go, Alyssa! Go!"

Alyssa grabbed the rope, swung over a ditch, and leaped over a series of logs to a ladder. It was bunk 6B versus 5C, and Alyssa was the last one up on the obstacle course.

Normally the obstacle course was not Alyssa's thing—not at all. It was definitely more of an Alex or Jenna type activity. Alyssa liked to observe nature and be a part of it, not conquer it.

But that afternoon she felt energized, as if a surge of electricity was running through her arms and legs. She didn't know what was causing it, but she was running the obstacle course of her life.

"One hand over the other!" Alex shouted. "You can do it, Alyssa!"

Alyssa dangled over the ground, crossing a set of monkey bars hand over hand. She'd have blisters later, but she didn't care. Bunk 6B had to beat 5C. The sixth-division girls were a year older, after all. They had their pride.

The bars seemed to jump into her hands. Alyssa almost felt as if she didn't have to do anything—her body was guided by an invisible force. She jumped off the monkey bars and raced for the finish line. Mandy waited there with a timer. The other girls were jumping up and down and screaming.

"Five point three minutes!" Mandy announced. "The fastest time today! Sixth division wins!"

Alyssa's bunkmates circled her and smothered her with hugs. Alyssa felt like she was dreaming. She'd never been the star of an athletic event before, or helped her team win. It was almost . . . eerie.

"All right, Alyssa!" Jenna said.

"Have you been working out or something?" Valerie said. "I've never seen you run like that."

"I know," Alyssa said. "It's weird, isn't it?" She wiped a bead of sweat from her brow with the back of her hand and considered what Valerie had just said.

"Yeah," Candace said. "It *is* kind of weird, now that you mention it."

Mandy led the girls back to the beginning of the obstacle course. Alyssa was still panting, but she felt great. Jenna draped an arm over her shoulders in sporty solidarity.

Mandy tucked her clipboard under her arm. "Maybe you're developing new skills as you get older," she said. "That's natural."

"Maybe," Alyssa said. "I always thought my artistic skills would improve, but I figured sports were a lost cause."

"You never know," Mandy said. "Anyway, everyone in the bunk gets a free can of soda, and Alyssa, for your stellar performance, you win an extra prize: a free makeover with Counselor Yvette."

"You're so lucky," Chelsea said. "I heard Yvette's a real professional makeup artist."

"Great!" Alyssa said. She hadn't been expecting to win anything, and she wasn't all that into makeup and stuff, but why not?

The girls from 5C met them at the head of the course to shake hands. "Nice job," a 5C-er named Winnie said. "But there are more challenges coming up. How about a swim relay, girls? Thank you can handle it?"

"And maybe you'd better lock your bunk door," said another 5C girl.

"What's that supposed to mean?" Brynn said.

"The bunk doors don't lock," Candace said.

The 5C girls just giggled and walked away,

whispering. The 6B-ers lingered, watching them go.

"What do you think they meant by that?" Alyssa said.

"I'm not sure," Jenna said. "But I don't like the sound of it. Sounds like they're planning a prank."

"A prank?" Sloan said. "What kind of prank?"

"You sneak into a rival bunk and put shaving cream on the toilet seats, run their panties up the flagpole, replace their secret candy stash with acorns," Jenna said. "That sort of thing."

"Jenna used to be Queen of the Pranks," Alex said.

"Pranking can get out of hand fast," Mandy said. "I don't want our bunk involved in anything like that."

"We wouldn't think of it," Chelsea said. "But those 5C girls as good as threatened us!"

"I wouldn't worry about it," Mandy said. "They're just teasing. And maybe they're sore losers. Good job today, girls. Especially you, Alyssa. I had no idea you were such a jock."

"I'm totally not," Alyssa said. "Not usually. I swear."

"Let's get back to the bunk," Mandy said. "Natalie's waiting."

"Hey, maybe she'll have some good news from her mother," Alyssa said. She hoped her prediction had been right and Tumtum was okay. Mostly for Natalie and Tumtum's sake, but also, just a little bit, to prove that she, Alyssa, really was psychic.

So far this had been one of the greatest days of her life. Not that anything big had happened, but the energy of the universe seemed to be flowing in her direction. Everything was going right. She'd had the best breakfast in Lakeview history, she got her first choice electives, did better than she thought on her swimming test, and won the obstacle course practically single-handedly. Amazing!

▲ ▲ ▲

As soon as Alyssa walked through the door, Natalie jumped up and threw her arms around her.

"The tumor was benign," Natalie said. "Tumtum's going to be okay!"

"Hurray!" All the girls cheered.

Alyssa hugged Natalie. She was thrilled. "This day just keeps getting better and better!" she said.

"Alyssa—you were right!" Natalie said. "How did you know Tumtum would be okay?"

Alyssa shrugged. "I don't really know. I just had a feeling."

The girls grew quiet. "You had a feeling. That's weird," Candace said. "Alyssa's been right about everything today."

"Yeah," Valerie said. "She's on a hot streak."

"It's the amethyst," Sloan said.

"It must be," Natalie said. "Alyssa was always kind of intuitive, but now she's, like, supernatural. The amethyst must be giving her more psychic ability."

Alyssa took the stone out of her shoe and looked at it. All the girls did.

"Do you really think that stone has powers?" Valerie said.

"I do," Alyssa said. "Since I found this amethyst, my life has completely changed. I've had nothing but good luck today. It's like . . . like magic."

"That's ridiculous," Chelsea said. "You just made a few lucky guesses. If you'd asked me, I would have said Natalie's dog would be okay, too."

"Still," Alyssa said. "Maybe we should keep quiet about the amethyst. I mean, let's not say anything to anyone outside the bunk. In case there's something to it."

Truth be told, Alyssa had no doubt that there *was* something to the amethyst's magic. But she didn't want to say so too firmly without more proof. She was afraid she'd sound nutty, and more teasing from Chelsea was the last thing she needed.

"Alyssa has a point," Jenna said. "If other kids find out that we have a magic amethyst, they might try to steal it as part of a prank. You heard what those girls from 5C said."

"That's true," Alex said. "They might have been kidding around, but if those girls hear about this, they might actually do something."

"Do something?" Candace said. "Like what?"

"We could wake up one morning to find toothpaste in our shoes," Jenna said. "For starters."

"Ick! No," Chelsea said.

"This prank business wasn't in the camp brochure," Sloan said.

"Maybe we *should* keep the amethyst a secret," Alex said.

"I agree," Brynn said. "That rock is pretty powerful."

"Let's swear," Alyssa said. "Let's superswear." The girls gathered in a circle and linked their pinkies together. "All right—we all swear to keep the existence of this amethyst a solemn secret. We swear to tell no one outside this cabin. Swear?"

Everyone said "We swear" in unison.

"Superswear?" Alyssa said.

"Superswear." They shook their linked pinkies once, twice, three times, and then let go.

"Remember—anyone who breaks a superswear will be cursed for the rest of the summer," Alyssa said. "So we're agreed: The amethyst is a secret."

She gazed fondly at the stone. She was getting very attached to it—almost like a security blanket.

When she was little, Alyssa had named her blanket Bluie, because it was blue. Not very original, but she was only three at the time. Maybe the amethyst deserved a name of its own, too.

"I have one more little ceremony I'd like to perform," Alyssa said.

"I know," Sloan said. "Putting a hex on 5C?"

"No," Alyssa said. "That's a good idea, though. Maybe later." She glanced around the room. "Does anybody have a wand?"

"A wand?" Gaby said. "Who brings a wand to summer camp?"

Alyssa went into the bathroom and grabbed a Q-tip. She dipped it in a bottle of pink nail polish to make it look like something besides an ordinary Q-tip. Okay, it looked like a Q-tip dipped in pink nail polish, but it would have to do . . .

"That's your wand?" Sloan said.

"Does anybody have something better I can use?" Alyssa asked. "I didn't think so." She waved the Q-tip over the amethyst, chanting, "I hereby dub thee . . ." She paused, trying to think of a good name.

"Hermione?" Brynn said.

"Alyssa junior?" Jenna said.

"Chip?" Chelsea said.

None of those names felt right. "Amy," Alyssa said. Amy the Amethyst sounded kind of like Bluie the Blanket. "I hereby dub thee Amy." She tapped the stone with the wand three times.

"Amy?" Gaby said. "You're naming your rock Amy?"

"Why not?" Alyssa said. "I'm getting attached to her. She needs a name. Besides, I think it suits her."

"Her?" Chelsea said. "Alyssa, it's a *piece of stone*."

"And she's my constant companion," Alyssa said.

▲ ▲ ▲

From then on, Alyssa tried to take Amy with her wherever she went, but carrying the stone was inconvenient. It made an unsightly bulge in her shorts pocket, and if she held it in her hand, she couldn't participate in her activities. And she was afraid of losing it on one of the trails or leaving it on her beach towel or something. So, right before dinner, Alyssa decided she needed a hiding place for Amy. A good one, not something obvious like the inside of her sneaker.

And, just to be safe, she wouldn't let anyone know where Amy was hidden. Not even her bunkmates. Not even Natalie.

When it was time to go to the mess hall for dinner, Alyssa held back. "Alyssa, Chelsea, let's move," Mandy said. "You'll be late for dinner."

"I can't get this purple eye shadow right," Chelsea said. She was stationed in front of the bathroom mirror, focused intently on her eye makeup.

Alyssa rolled her eyes. She wished Chelsea would hurry up and leave so she could hide Amy without being seen.

"I'll be right there," Alyssa said. "I can't find one of my flip-flops." She was sitting on the "lost" flip-flop, waiting for everyone to leave.

"You go ahead, Alyssa," Chelsea said. "I'll catch up."

"I can't go to the mess hall barefoot," Alyssa said.

"So wear your sneakers," Chelsea said. "What's the big deal?"

What's the big deal with purple eye shadow? Alyssa thought, but she didn't say it out loud.

Mandy's face appeared in one of the windows. "Girls. Let's go."

"Ugh." Chelsea put down her makeup brush in disgust. "I give up. Come on, Alyssa."

"One sec. I'll catch up." Chelsea flounced out of the cabin at last. Alyssa waited until Chelsea was out of sight. Then she climbed up onto her top bunk. She'd thought of the perfect hiding place for Amy. Even if some evil campers decided to prank them and totally ransacked the cabin, they'd never find Amy.

Alyssa's bunk bed was right next to the window. She opened the screen and reached outside. There was a little nook behind the shutter on the outside wall of the cabin that might have once held a flagpole or something. It was just the right size for Amy. And with the shutter open and hiding the spot, no one would ever notice that the rock was there. And even if someone knew about it, who would think to look for it *outside* the cabin?

Pleased with her cleverness, Alyssa put on her flip-flops and left for dinner, satisfied that her magic amethyst would be safe and sound.

chapter FOUR

"Good morning, Star Children." Alyssa woke up in a good mood. She pulled Amy the Amethyst out from under her pillow, where Amy would both prevent nightmares and stay securely out of any pranksters' hands. "And how are everybody's spirits this morning?"

"Star Children? Please, don't start with that crunchy stuff so early," Chelsea moaned. "Unless that amethyst can tell me how to prevent split ends and make my stomach flatter, I don't want to hear about it."

"I do," Brynn said. "Alyssa, I need your help. Can you use Amy to read Jordan's mind? Please? I'm dying to know if we're going to get back together, but I can't tell what he's thinking."

"Make Amy tell me how to win over Donovan," Gaby said. "What kind of girl does he like? Should I dye my hair blond? Start wearing kneesocks? What?"

"Can Amy predict whether my team will win the volleyball game today?" Alex asked.

Alyssa clutched Amy, trying to absorb her

bunkmates' questions and the universe's answers. "Slow down," she said. "I'm getting nothing but static."

"You can't just throw questions at an amethyst," Sloan said. "You have to choose carefully, and give Alyssa time to read the answer. She can't try to predict everything at once or she'll get confusing signals."

"Thank you, Sloan," Alyssa said.

"Let's get dressed, girls," Mandy said. "Breakfast starts in ten minutes."

"Just make one prediction before breakfast," Brynn said.

"All right," Alyssa said. "I'll predict what we're having for breakfast today." She closed her eyes and breathed deeply. An image appeared in her mind: a plate, butter, syrup, pancakes. Yes, the image of pancakes was so strong, she could practically smell them.

She opened her eyes. "Pancakes," she announced. "Today we're having pancakes."

"I don't care what we're having," Mandy said. "If you want to eat anything at all this morning, you better get a move on."

Alyssa dressed quickly. When everyone had left the cabin, she quickly slipped Amy into her hiding spot. Then she ran outside and caught up with her bunkmates. As they walked up the path toward the mess hall, Brynn sniffed and said, "You know what? I think I smell pancakes."

Candace opened the door and they stepped inside the dining hall. The smell of pancakes filled the room. As confirmation, a CIT set a big platter of pancakes and sausages on one of the tables.

"Wow," Candace said. "Alyssa, you were right again!"

"That's incredible!" Gaby said.

"You really have a gift," Sloan said.

Even Alyssa was amazed. She'd never made so many predictions correctly before. Amy truly was magic.

"Welcome to nature," Roseanne said. Tall, with hair in long, crazy curls, she was an earth-mother type and the perfect nature counselor. "We'll be studying the natural world in all its glory, both the facts that we know as scientists, and the mysteries that awe us."

Excellent, Alyssa thought. *The mysteries of nature.* Those mysteries interested her a lot now, because Amy's power struck her as both a fact and an inexplicable phenomenon, a mystery she hoped to understand better.

A chubby girl with a close-cut Afro and glasses raised her hand. "Roseanne?"

"Yes, Gwenda?"

"Are there really any mysteries to nature?" Gwenda said. "I mean, aren't mysteries really just facts that we don't know yet?"

What kind of person thinks that way? Alyssa thought. *Reducing awe-inspiring mysteries to a bunch of facts?* She recognized Gwenda as a fifth-division girl, but she didn't know her.

"Good point, Gwenda," Roseanne said. "That's certainly one way to look at it. I'm not sure we can ever know all the facts. The mysteries are what make nature so fascinating. But this is an issue we could argue about for a long time."

"I don't see any argument," Gwenda said. "Science always moves us forward. In the future people will understand the things that seem mysterious to us. It's only a matter of time."

"Wow, geek city," Priya whispered to Alyssa. "I'd introduce myself to her except I don't know how to say hello in Robot."

"Before we get started," Roseanne said, "I want to announce that later in the summer we'll be holding a nature fair with exhibits from campers about any aspects of nature that interest them. So if you plan to be in nature again next session, you should think about what you'd like to exhibit at your table."

As Gwenda dutifully wrote this down in a notebook, Alyssa wondered what her exhibit would be. Probably something uber-brainy, like a demonstration of astrophysics.

I wonder if there's some way I could exhibit Amy and her powers, Alyssa thought. That was certainly shaping up to be a wonder of nature.

"Let's start by looking at some of the local terrain," Roseanne said. She held up a pale purplish-blue plant Alyssa immediately recognized. "Here's something you might find growing in the mountains in this area. Who can tell me what it is?"

Alyssa and Gwenda both raised their hands. Roseanne called on Alyssa.

"Lavender," Alyssa said.

"That's right," Roseanne said. "What can you tell me about lavender?"

"Well, it's an herb," Alyssa said. "Some people believe it keeps away the evil eye. And if you give it to a friend, it helps her stay loyal to you. It's also good for insect bites."

"Good," Roseanne said. "Anything else?"

Gwenda raised her hand. "Lavender grows best with lots of sun and low humidity, in slightly salty soil."

"Very good," Roseanne said.

Low humidity? Alyssa thought. *Who cares about that when you're talking about one of the most powerful herbs of all time? You can practically make love potions out of the stuff, and Gwenda's talking about low humidity. I'll never understand science people.*

Roseanne talked about other plants and trees and flowers that grow in Pennsylvania. Gwenda knew scientific facts about all of them. Alyssa knew their mystical and healing properties. Then Roseanne moved on to rocks and minerals. "Western Pennsylvania is still a major mining area," she said. "People even prospected for silver near here." She held up a rough piece of hammered silver.

"Ooh! Ooh!" Gwenda could barely stay in her seat. "Silver's elemental symbol is Ag on the periodic table. Silver has the highest electrical and thermal conductivity of all metals."

"Holy moly," Alyssa whispered to Priya. "This girl is like a walking encyclopedia."

"Wow," Roseanne said. "We've got a real science whiz in this group. Does anyone have anything they want to add?"

"Lots of people think silver mirrors the soul,"

Alyssa said. "It's related to the moon and connects us to the planets and stars."

Roseanne stared at her. Everyone in the group stared at both Alyssa and Gwenda as if they were freaks. *Sure,* Alyssa thought, *Gwenda's practically from another planet. But I'm totally normal.* Still, the way the group looked at her made her uncomfortable. Her own words echoed in her head. Had she said something weird?

"Lighten up, you guys," a boy said. "It's just metal."

"I've never had such well-informed campers in my nature group," Roseanne said. "This session should be very enlightening. Okay, you're free to go. Remember to keep an eye out for all the wonderful plants and minerals around you, and we'll talk about what you find tomorrow."

Gwenda got up from her seat and stopped by Alyssa's on her way out. "Your contributions to the discussion were fascinating, but irrelevant," Gwenda said, while Priya looked on. "You realize that none of the properties you mentioned have been proven by any reputable scientist, don't you?"

"People have believed them for centuries," Alyssa said. "Science doesn't prove everything."

Gwenda snorted. "Science is the *only* way to prove *anything*. Duh. See you tomorrow."

"See you, Mr. Spock," Alyssa said to Priya after Gwenda left. "Did you ever meet such a science lunatic?"

"No," Priya said. "But I never met anyone as superstitious as you, either. I think you're both crazy."

"Hmph," Alyssa said. "I'm not crazy—I'm psychic! That's totally different."

▲ ▲ ▲

"Head into the wind. Into the wind, Gaby!" Hank, the sailing instructor, had been shouting at Gaby all afternoon. What did he expect? She'd never sailed before, or not much, anyway. So it was no surprise that she capsized about a hundred times and couldn't figure out which way to push the tiller or which rope tightened the mainsail and which the jib.

"I'm soaked," Valerie said. She had agreed to be Gaby's sailing partner, just for the first day. "And no, I *don't* want to take another involuntary dip in the lake. Maybe we should head in."

"Aye, aye, Captain." Gaby let Valerie take the tiller at last. Valerie steered them awkwardly but steadily toward the dock.

Hank called all the sailors back to dry land for a talk. Gaby watched with envy as Candace expertly tied her boat to the pier. Donovan was already sitting on the dock, talking to some blond girl from the fifth division. To Gaby's disappointment, the blonde had asked to be his partner, and he'd said yes. Gaby hoped the partnerships weren't permanent. Valerie was okay, but Gaby hadn't signed up for sailing to become better friends with a *girl*.

Gaby and Valerie joined Candace on the dock. "The girls are all over Donovan," Valerie whispered. "Today alone I saw Chelsea eating lunch with him and some fourth-division girl interrupting his tennis match to ask him to volley with her. Now blondie here."

"All right, sailors, this was a good first day," Hank said. "I see we have a lot of experienced sailors and a fair number of rookies. This first sailing session will end with a big regatta a month from now, with each boat sailed by a skipper and a first mate. I thought I'd pair up the new sailors with the old hands to make the race more fair. Sound good?"

Everyone nodded, especially Gaby. If she'd proven anything that day, it was that she did not know how to sail. Which meant she'd be paired with a pro, like, say, Donovan, perhaps? She crossed her fingers.

"Here are the teams," Hank said, reading from his clipboard. "Candace, you'll be a skipper, and Valerie, you'll be first mate."

"Yes!" Valerie and Candace high-fived.

"Tom, skipper," Hank said. "Alaric, first mate."

Hank read off a few more names. Gaby got more and more nervous, waiting for her name to be called. *Please please please . . .*

"Donovan, skipper, with Gaby, first mate," Hank read.

Yes! Gaby tried to hide her excitement. She looked at Donovan and nodded soberly. He grinned at her.

Ooh, that grin . . . For once luck was going Gaby's way. Sailing was going to be awesome.

When the meeting was over, Gaby got up to go talk to Donovan—she figured they had a lot of sailing partner issues to discuss, perhaps over ice cream sundaes that evening? But before she had a chance to stop him, the blond girl pulled him away. Oh well. There was always the next day. If there was one thing Gaby was happily sure about now, it was that from now on she'd have access to Donovan no matter what.

▲ ▲ ▲

"I think every night should be Make Your Own Sundae night," Brynn said.

"Totally," Gaby said. The girls of bunk 6B were wolfing down their chicken cutlets so they could hit the ice cream buffet. Gaby had been watching Donovan all through dinner. He sat with his bunk, but now he'd bussed his tray and was waylaid on his way back to his table by a group of giggling girls. After a few minutes, he managed to extract himself from them and continue on his way across the mess hall.

Brynn elbowed Gaby. "Look who's coming this way."

Donovan was headed right for them. *At last,* Gaby thought. "Did I tell you he's going to be my sailing partner?" she said to Brynn. "I'm his first mate."

"You already told us," Brynn said. "About a thousand times."

Donovan had almost reached their table when Priya intercepted him. Gaby watched as Priya pointed to the ice cream station and led Donovan over there.

"Priya cut him off!" Gaby cried. She was indignant. How dare Priya do that? "Look—they're making sundaes together!"

Gaby gritted her teeth while Priya and Donovan scooped ice cream into their bowls and poured hot fudge on top.

"Now they're headed outside," Brynn said. "They'll probably eat their sundaes at one of the picnic tables."

"How romantic," Gaby grumbled. "I called dibs."

"You can't call dibs on a boy," Brynn said. "Didn't anyone ever tell you that, Gaby?"

"Yes," Gaby said. "Valerie did. At the cookout, remember?"

"Oh, yeah," Brynn said. "I thought those words sounded familiar."

"I don't know who made up that rule," Gaby said. "I can call dibs on a boy if I want."

"But it won't get you much," Brynn said.

"I'm just saying we girls should stick together," Gaby said. "Priya and I are bunkmates. Everybody knows I like Donovan. I'm his first mate, even, so all others should back off."

"All the girls are after him," Brynn said. "Why should Priya back off? He could like any one of them. You may be his first mate, but you're not his girlfriend."

"Yet," Gaby said.

Brynn rolled her eyes.

"I saw that," Gaby said.

"Let's get some ice cream," Brynn said.

Gaby followed her to the ice cream station. She took two scoops of chocolate and smothered them in chocolate sauce. "Donovan may be flitting around, but he can only ask one girl to the Midsummer Dance."

Brynn sprinkled walnuts into her bowl and squirted whipped cream on top. "You're right, Gaby.

He can only take one girl to the dance. And Priya just put herself in the running."

"That's just not fair," Gaby said. "I'm his first mate. He's mine."

"Tell it to the judge," Brynn said. "Whoops. There is no judge. Sorry."

That night, Alyssa took Amy out of her hiding place before the rest of the bunk came back from dinner. She rubbed the rough patches on the stone and stared in wonder at the smooth, shiny purple spots. Already she'd rubbed the amethyst so much that it felt warm. Alyssa thought she could feel Amy transmitting psychic power to her through the skin of her palm.

Her bunkmates trooped in one by one to get ready for bed. Everyone changed into their pajamas and settled down for the night. *Someone's missing,* Alyssa thought. She checked all the beds and realized it was Priya.

"You know what's lame about Make Your Own Sundae night?" Candace said. "They never have my favorite flavor, pistachio."

"Pistachio is your favorite flavor?" Alex said.

"Yeah. So?" Candace said.

"No one's favorite ice cream is pistachio," Jenna said.

"No one's favorite is pistachio? That's obviously not true," Candace said. "Because mine is."

"I like pistachio, too, Candace," Tori said.

"But it's not your favorite, right?" Alex said.

"No, it's not my *favorite* . . ." Tori said. "Spumoni is my favorite."

"Spumoni! Ew!" Jenna said. "That's worse than pistachio!"

Everyone was already getting into pajamas when Priya finally arrived.

"So? How was it?" Gaby snapped at Priya.

"How was what?" Valerie asked.

"Priya and Donovan shared hot fudge sundaes," Brynn explained.

"They did?" Valerie said.

"Didn't you see them?" Brynn said. "They were outside at one of the picnic tables laughing their heads off."

"Really?" Valerie looked a little hurt. "Huh."

"What?" Gaby said. "What does 'huh' mean?"

"Nothing," Valerie said. "It's just that I asked Donovan to go on a nature walk after lunch tomorrow—"

"You did?" Gaby interrupted. "Everybody is after him! How will I ever get a chance to ask him to do anything if you all keep booking him up?"

"How was the sundae, Priya?" Valerie asked.

"Great," Priya said. "I did a fruit and nut combo: strawberry ice cream *only*, with strawberry sauce, walnuts, and a couple of cherries—"

"We don't care about your stupid sundae," Chelsea said. Then she quickly changed her tone. "I mean, that's nice, but we want to hear the part about Donovan."

"Oh. He's really nice. He asked me a lot of questions about camp and about myself . . . We talked about what songs we have on our iPods."

"What songs does he have?" Gaby asked.

"Um . . . I can't remember," Priya said.

"You're no help," Gaby said.

"I'm not trying to be," Priya said.

"Doesn't that guy ever say no?" Gaby said. "Alyssa, this is driving me crazy."

"It's driving us all crazy," Valerie said. "Donovan is leading everybody on. If only we knew who he really liked, we could try to stop thinking about him."

"Maybe he really likes everyone," Brynn said. "Or he doesn't really like anyone."

"Why don't you ask Amy?" Natalie said.

"Yeah," Gaby said. "What does the amethyst say? Predict the future for us, O Great Swamalyssa! Who will Donovan ask to the dance?"

"All right, I will." Alyssa closed her eyes and rubbed Amy between her fingers. She pictured Donovan in her mind, surrounded by girls, laughing and having fun with all of them. He turned from one to the next, but none of them stood out. As far as Alyssa could see, he liked them all. Then the picture grew hazy, as if a fog had drifted through the scene.

"What do you see?" Valerie asked.

"It's a little cloudy," Alyssa said, keeping her eyes closed. "But the message I'm getting is that Donovan wants to get to know everyone. He's new. He wants to be sure he makes the right choice."

"Ugh," Chelsea said. "I knew that stupid rock wouldn't work."

"Wait," Sloan said. "Give it time."

"Think, Alyssa," Gaby said.

Alyssa concentrated harder. She tried to picture Donovan at the Midsummer Dance. She saw him standing on the lawn outside the main lodge, which was decorated with flowers and balloons and flashing lights. Who was he with? Again she saw him circled by girls. One by one the girls disappeared, until Donovan stood alone. Then he reached out his hand, and offered it to . . . Candace.

Alyssa opened her eyes. Everyone gathered around her.

"What? What did you see?" they asked.

Alyssa cleared her throat. She had a prediction to make, but she was afraid it wouldn't go over well. No matter what she said, somebody would get mad. But she had a duty to tell the future as she saw it.

"Tell us!" Gaby said.

"I'll tell you," Alyssa said. "But I want to make it clear that I have no personal preference. I'm just reporting the visions I see as Amy sends them to me. Okay?"

"Just tell us, for Pete's sake!" Chelsea snapped.

"Okay," Alyssa said. "Here's my prediction: The girl Donovan will ask to the dance is . . . Candace."

Everyone gasped.

"What?" Gaby cried.

"Candace?" Chelsea said.

"Me?" Candace said. "But I haven't done anything to make him like me. I've barely even talked to the guy."

Alyssa shrugged. "What can I say? Amy has spoken."

"But—I can't go to the dance with him," Candace

said. "I'm boy-free this summer, remember?"

"And you should stay that way." Gaby patted Candace on the shoulder. "Good for you, Candace."

"Are you sure, Alyssa?" Valerie asked.

Alyssa nodded. "Don't blame me. I'm just channeling Amy."

"I don't believe it," Gaby said.

"This is ridiculous," Chelsea said. "That amethyst can't tell us what Donovan will or will not do. We shouldn't listen to it. I say it's wrong."

"I don't know," Natalie said. "Alyssa's been right about an awful lot of stuff lately. Weirdly right."

"She has the gift," Sloan said. "Anyone can see that."

Mandy came out of the bathroom and sat down on her bed in the little counselor's nook. Alyssa realized she'd been quietly listening all along. "I'm with Chelsea," Mandy said. "The amethyst is fun, but we shouldn't put too much stock in it. We certainly shouldn't let it run our lives. So, Alyssa—did Amy say anything about it being lights out?"

Everyone crawled into bed with her own thoughts. Alyssa climbed into her top bunk and put Amy under her pillow.

"Good night, girls," Mandy said.

She turned out the light, but Alyssa lay awake with her eyes open. The amethyst's power was real. She could feel it. Amy wasn't ridiculous. And if she could predict the future, how could that not affect their lives?

chapter FIVE

"So I'm standing in the hall at school, screaming at the top of my lungs, and no one can hear me," Brynn said. She was telling Alyssa about the dream she'd just had. As soon as Alyssa opened her eyes that morning, her bunkmates started demanding dream interpretations. Alyssa brushed her teeth, holding Amy in one hand and listening to Brynn in the bathroom.

"And I'm walking around school, and everybody looks right through me," Brynn said. "It's like I'm invisible. No one can see me or hear me. I'm singing and shouting and dancing around like a nut, but no one notices. It was so frustrating! What does it mean?"

Alyssa spit out her toothpaste, rinsed her mouth, and went back into the bunk room, trailed by Brynn. She rubbed Amy, but she didn't need to close her eyes for this dream interpretation.

"Here's what your dream means," she said to Brynn. "You crave attention."

Chelsea laughed. "Big stretch. Brynn is the empress of the drama queens. She craves attention? I could have told her that."

"Still, Alyssa's right," Brynn said. "I do like attention. That's one reason I want to be an actress."

"Alyssa, do my dream," Tori said. "I line up all my nail polish colors in a row, by color, from dark to light, with sparkly polishes last. But just as I'm setting the last bottle down, a giant hand reaches down from the sky and knocks them all over like bowling pins! I set them all up again, but the hand keeps knocking them down. By the end of the dream I'm crying."

"Hmm." Alyssa pulled on her shorts, and then sat down for a consultation with Amy. "Your dream means that the world is too messy for you. You wish everything could be neat and orderly."

"Wow." Tori shook her head, impressed. "That's genius. Pure genius."

"Okay, girls, that's enough dream interpretation for now," Mandy said. "We've got some other important things to talk about this morning—like the swim relay against bunk 5C this afternoon. How are we going to beat them?"

Amy seemed to warm up in Alyssa's hand, and something made her look out the window. The sun was shining, but clouds loomed in the distance.

"No point talking about swim meets," she said. "The relay race will be canceled because of rain."

"Oh, no," Jenna said. "No race?"

"You want to hear my prediction?" Mandy said. "I predict that if we're not dressed in five minutes, we're going to miss breakfast." She clapped her hands, and everyone scurried to get dressed. No one wanted to miss breakfast. Even Alyssa had to admit that if they didn't hurry, Mandy's prediction would probably come true.

"Here I am, Skipper, reporting for duty." The sailors gathered on the dock after breakfast. Gaby gave Donovan a neat salute. She had prepared for their first day as a sailing team by putting on a striped sailor top over her best navy shorts. Tori had helped her French braid her hair, and she'd loaded up on blush, aqua blue eye shadow (to help her eyes reflect the color of the water), rose petal lip gloss, and a ton of mascara.

Donovan glanced at her. "Uh, okay. At ease, dude. I mean, mate."

Gaby slouched in an attempt to look comfortable. She wasn't sure what Donovan meant by "at ease," but figured it must have something to do with looking relaxed.

"All right, sailors," Hank said. "Everybody aboard your boats, and let's practice going about."

"Going about what?" Gaby asked.

"Just 'going about,'" Donovan said. "It's a sailing term."

"It refers to your boat changing direction," Candace said.

"Right," Donovan said.

"Oh." Gaby watched Candace and Valerie climb into their Sunfish. Candace showed Valerie how to untie the knot that held the boat to the dock. Next to them, Logan helped the little bowl-haired kid, Alaric, into their boat before they scooted out over the lake.

Donovan held their boat steady for Gaby as she climbed in.

"Here." Donovan tossed her a lumpy, ugly

orange life jacket. "Better put that on."

She sighed, but she put it on, even though it completely ruined her look. Donovan buckled his on, too. "Okay," he said. "Pull up the jib."

Gaby looked around. What was the jib again? She was afraid to ask him, because then he'd know how totally clueless she was on a boat. So she tugged on the first line she found.

"Dude, not the bowsprit," Donovan said. "The jib."

She gave him a blank look. She couldn't help it. Bowsprit? Jib? It was like he was speaking a foreign language.

He laughed. "Here." He handed her a rope. "The jib is the small sail up front. Pull this and the jib will slide up the mast."

"Oh. I knew that," Gaby said. She pulled on the rope and, just as he'd said, the small sail rose up the mast.

"Now cleat it here." Donovan showed her a funny little clamp. She put the rope between the two serrated edges and the clamp held it still. "Good. Do you know how to tie a slipknot?"

"Um . . . no."

"Here, I'll show you." He showed her how to tie a simple knot. Maybe being clueless would work to her advantage. He had to pay a lot more attention to her if she didn't know what she was doing.

He pulled up the mainsail and they started out onto the lake. There was a light breeze.

"Okay, first mate," he said. "When I say, 'Ready about!' you get ready. Then I'll say, 'Hard a-lee!' I'll push the tiller all the way out like this—" He pushed the bar that steered the boat far out to the right. "And you duck. Because the boom will swing around and you don't want it to hit you in the head. Got it?"

"Got it." She had no idea what he was talking about. A bit farther out, Candace and Valerie tacked smoothly from side to side.

"See Candace out there?" Donovan said. "She's doing it right."

Gaby squinted into the sun, trying to figure out exactly what Candace was doing.

"Let's pick up a little speed . . ." Donovan steered the boat so the breeze filled the sails. Soon they were zipping across the lake.

"Hey, this is fun," Gaby said.

Donovan grinned. "It is, right? Okay, ready to go about?"

"Ready."

"Ready about—hard a-lee!"

Gaby ducked. The Sunfish stalled, and the boom swung over her head as the boat turned around. Soon they were sailing fast again, but Gaby was afraid to come up.

"Is it safe yet?" she asked.

"Yes, it's safe," Donovan said. "Come up, quick. I need you to tighten the jib."

At least she knew what the jib was now. She picked up the rope she'd cleated and gave it a tug.

"Good. You're getting the hang of it, mate," Donovan said.

Candace and Valerie swooped past them, then neatly turned around.

"That chick knows her way around a boat, doesn't she?" Donovan nodded at Candace's boat.

"I guess," Gaby said.

"Ahoy there!" He called to Candace, waving his arm. "Want to race?"

"Sure!" Candace shouted back. "Once around the buoy?" She pointed to an orange ball, a marker, floating in the lake.

"And back to the first marker." Donovan nodded at a red flag waving a few feet off the dock. "Ready to beat these girls?" he asked Gaby.

"Totally ready," Gaby said.

Candace slowed her Sunfish slightly until the two boats were about even. Then Valerie shouted, "On your mark, get set, go!" and they were off.

Donovan tightened the sails and they leaped ahead of Candace and Valerie. Gaby felt the wind pushing them across the water. "Let out the jib a little," Donovan said. Gaby loosened the jib line and let the sail flap in the wind. "Not too much!" Donovan snapped. Gaby made a face at him—she couldn't help it, it was involuntary—and tightened the sail. He was a slightly cranky skipper.

Candace was gaining on them, but Gaby's boat still had the lead. They reached the orange buoy and were preparing to go around it. "Ready about?" Donovan said.

Gaby got ready to duck. But Tom's boat suddenly darted in front of them—Alaric was steering. Donovan had to change direction quickly or they'd crash. He slammed the tiller to the left. The boom swung around and knocked Gaby off the boat. She flew through the air and splashed into the lake.

"Whoa!" She sank into the water, but quickly bobbed to the surface, thanks to her life jacket. She sputtered and wiped the wet hair from her eyes.

"Sorry about that!" Tom waved as he took over for Alaric.

"Are you all right?" Donovan asked.

"Fine," Gaby said. "Great!" Inside she was burning mad. But she was determined not to show it, to be a good sport. She'd just blown the race—and it was stupid Tom's fault. Or that kid Alaric's. Whoever. It didn't matter—she felt like a jerk.

Gaby bobbed and floated in the lake. "I'll be right there to pick you up," Donovan called, but at that moment his boat was pointed in the other direction, moving away from her. He headed into the wind to stop it.

Candace and Valerie neatly tacked over to Gaby, Candace at the helm. "I've got her!" she called, giving Donovan a wave. Valerie reached out and grabbed Gaby's arm to help pull her into the boat.

"Way to make a splash," Valerie said. Then she looked at Gaby's face and laughed. Candace laughed, too.

"What?" Gaby said. "What's so funny?"

"What's so funny is your makeup," Candace said.

"What about my makeup?" Gaby looked desperately around for some kind of shiny surface so she could check her reflection, but there was nothing. Why didn't these stupid little boats come equipped with makeup mirrors? Better yet, built-in vanity tables?

More comfortable seating wouldn't hurt, either. A lounge chair would be nice . . .

Candace and Valerie were still laughing. "What's wrong with my makeup?" Gaby asked impatiently.

"Well . . ." Valerie said. "It's all smeared—"

"—and you look kind of like a clown," Candace said.

Gaby's hands flew to her face. She was horrified. "Like a clown! Don't let Donovan see me!" His boat was headed their way.

"Only *kind of* like a clown," Candace said.

"Yeah," Valerie said. "Kind of like a clown, and kind of like somebody shot you in the face with a paintball gun."

"No!" Gaby cried, desperately wiping makeup from her eyes.

"You shouldn't wear so much makeup to go sailing," Candace said. "People do end up in the water pretty often. And these little Sunfish capsize all the time."

"If you're going to overdo it, at least wear waterproof mascara," Valerie said.

Donovan's boat pulled up just then. "Come on, Gaby. Climb aboard."

Gaby turned her face away from him. "No."

"What? Why not?"

"Gaby, get off our boat," Valerie said. "There really isn't room for three on this thing."

"No," Gaby said, hiding her face with her hands.

"Gaby, get back on here," Donovan said. "That's an order."

"You're not the boss of me," Gaby said. She knew it sounded babyish, but that's how she felt just then. She wished she could snap her fingers and disappear.

"Come on, Gaby," Candace whispered to her. "You don't look so bad. Lighten up. Have a sense of humor. It's funny."

Gaby let her hands drop away from her face. She stuck out her tongue at Candace. Candace wouldn't think it was so funny if it happened to *her*. But no, of course something like this would never happen to Candace, since she was such a good sailor and all.

"Gaby, if you don't get back on this boat I'll consider it a mutiny," Donovan said. "And I'll have to find another first mate."

No, not that! Anything but that.

Gaby turned around slowly. Donovan reached out to help her. He took one look at her face and burst out laughing, even as he pulled her aboard their boat. "Wear makeup much?"

"Stop that!" Gaby said.

"It's just—" He was shaking with laughter. "You look like a clown . . ."

Gaby grimaced. "Can we just get back to the dock, please?"

Donovan pointed the boat toward shore. "Thanks for your help, Candace," he called over his shoulder. "Nice sailing! But we would have kicked your butts if it hadn't been for our little accident here."

So it was my fault, was it? Gaby fumed. She'd show him. She could be a great first mate. She just needed a few lessons.

"Don't worry, Gaby," Donovan said. "We'll beat them next time."

He confidently steered the Sunfish toward the dock. The wind blew back his dark mop of hair, exposing the shell necklace at his throat. Gaby sighed. She couldn't care less about beating Candace or anyone else in a race. All she cared about was how cute Donovan was.

But sailing was obviously not her strong suit. She needed to find another way to win Donovan over. The question was, how?

▲ ▲ ▲

After lunch the skies opened up and rain drenched the camp. "The swim relay is postponed," Mandy announced, avoiding Alyssa's eyes. Gaby snickered. Alyssa and Amy had been right again, but Mandy obviously didn't want to admit it.

"So you have a free period," Mandy said. "You can hang out in the main lodge if you want, or stay here in the bunk and read or write letters. Up to you. I'm going up to the lodge to work on a mural for the Midsummer Dance. Anybody who wants to come help is welcome."

Gaby watched to see what Alyssa would do. Alyssa reached under her pillow and pulled out Amy. "I think I'll stay here and read," she said.

"Me too," Gaby said. She had a little favor to ask Alyssa, and this was the perfect time.

Some of the girls left for the main lodge. Gaby, Alyssa, Sloan, and Natalie stayed in the cabin.

Gaby glanced up at Alyssa, lying on her top

bunk. Alyssa opened a book and started reading. Below her, Natalie lay on her stomach writing a letter. Across the room, Sloan sat on the floor, dealing tarot cards. Gaby stepped on Natalie's bed to climb up to Alyssa's.

"I need to talk to you," Gaby said.

Alyssa rolled over to make room for her. "Fire away."

"I don't know if you heard about my humiliation in sailing today . . ." Gaby began.

Alyssa laughed, and beneath them Natalie snickered.

"Guess that answers that question," Gaby said.

"Valerie and Candace told us," Alyssa said.

"It's nothing to be ashamed of," Natalie said. "I've been in the exact same situation. Well, almost exact. I fell into the lake with a face full of makeup on in front of Logan last year. My waterproof mascara totally saved me."

"Yeah, well, I didn't think that far ahead this morning," Gaby said.

"My point is, look where Logan and I ended up," Natalie said.

"Where *did* you end up?" Gaby asked. "Are you back together now?"

"No, not yet," Natalie admitted. "And I'm not sure if we will be or not this summer. I asked my Magic 8-Ball before I left for camp, but all it said was, *Reply hazy, try again.*"

"I told you, the Magic 8-Ball doesn't know what it's talking about," Alyssa said. "It's a toy. It's got no mojo."

"*Anyway,*" Natalie said, and Gaby could practically hear her rolling her eyes. "Last summer Logan and I did get together, even though I made a complete fool of myself in front of him. So all is not lost, Gaby."

"All I wanted was to look good for Donovan," Gaby said. "We're going to be spending a lot of time on a boat together, and I wanted to make a good impression."

"Maybe you should focus on being a good sailor instead of looking like a beauty queen," Alyssa said.

"But that's just the problem," Gaby said. "I'll never be a good sailor—not in the four weeks we have until the regatta, anyway. So I might as well forget about sailing as a way to Donovan's heart. I need another way. Alyssa, you've got to help me."

"Me? How can I help you?" Alyssa said.

Gaby cast her eyes toward the amethyst, which lay on the pillow next to Alyssa's head.

"What—Amy?" Alyssa said. She snatched Amy up and cradled her in her hand.

"Ask Amy what I should do," Gaby said. "Ask her what will make Donovan like me. You can do it. You're totally psychic now. You predicted this rainstorm. You predicted we'd have pancakes for breakfast and pasta salad at the cookout."

"She also predicted that Donovan will ask Candace to the Midsummer Dance," Natalie said.

"But maybe that could change," Gaby said. "If I can just get his attention somehow, in a good way . . ."

"I don't know," Alyssa said.

"Why not?" Gaby said.

"It just doesn't feel right," Alyssa said.

"Alyssa is right," Sloan said from her spot on the floor. She flipped over a tarot card—the hanging man. "She *is* totally psychic, but she shouldn't misuse it. If you use your power for selfish or evil reasons, it brings bad karma."

Gaby really wanted a boyfriend this summer, and she really liked Donovan. That may have been selfish, but wasn't it understandable? The others had all been in the same spot before, she was sure of it.

"This isn't evil, Sloan," Gaby said. "Please, Alyssa—help out a friend? Your bunkmate and fellow camper for all these years?" She batted her eyes at Alyssa and tried to smile her warmest smile. "It will only take a second. Just ask Amy what Donovan likes."

Alyssa shifted uncomfortably on her bed. "Sloan's right. I already asked who he'll ask to the dance. Isn't that enough of an answer for you?"

"Maybe something has happened since then to change the future," Gaby said. "It can't hurt to double-check."

"Sorry, Gaby," Alyssa said. "I can't double-check every prediction I make. Part of making predictions is trusting your first instincts."

"I'm not asking you to second-guess your instincts. Just to look for a possible new angle," Gaby said.

"I'll think about it," Alyssa said. "That's all I can promise."

"That's all I can ask," Gaby said. But she was determined. Somehow, some way, by the end of the summer, Donovan was going to be her boyfriend.

chapter
SIX

A few days later, Brynn went to the news-paper office to work. Drama and newspaper were her two electives. Drama she had down pat—they were doing *Anything Goes*, and tryouts were next week. But newspaper was troubling her. She was trying to think of something interesting to write about, but after so many years at camp, it all felt so familiar, so routine. There was nothing new, nothing exciting to report. Plus, it was a little awkward seeing Jordan—who was also a reporter—there.

When Brynn walked into the office, there he was, sitting at one of the computers and talking to a thin girl with a thick dark braid gleaming down her back—the fifth-division girl Brynn had seen him with at the cookout. Brynn remembered her from the obstacle course, too. They looked up at Brynn and immediately stopped talking, as if they didn't want her to hear their conversation.

"Hi, Brynn," Jordan said.

"Hi, Jordan," Brynn said. She smiled at the girl, even though she felt wary of her. "I'm Brynn."

"Winnie," the girl said. "Nice to meet you."

Brynn settled at one of the other computers. "What's new?" she asked Jordan. *What a lame question,* she thought, mentally kicking herself, but she didn't know what else to say.

"I'm starting a new column for the paper," Jordan said. "It's called Bunk Roundup. I'll give the latest news from each bunk, just a few lines for each. Unless something really big is happening. So what's going on in bunk 6B? Any news?"

"News?" All Brynn could think of was Alyssa and her amethyst. The predictions, the psychic powers. That was pretty big news. But she supersworE not to tell anyone about it. Alyssa said anyone who broke a superswear would be cursed. Brynn didn't need any bad luck. And the last person she should break a super-sworn secret to was a reporter from the camp paper. So she lied and said, "News? No, nothing. Nothing at all."

"Come on, it doesn't have to be earthshaking," Jordan said. "Just a little tidbit to round out the column. Otherwise the sixth-division girls won't be represented in Bunk Roundup."

Brynn racked her brain, trying to come up with some little bone she could throw to keep Jordan satisfied. "Well, we beat 5C in an obstacle course last week," she said. Then she remembered that Winnie was in 5C and regretted it. Winnie frowned. "Sorry. But it was kind of wild. Alyssa was the star—we totally couldn't have won without her."

"Alyssa?" Jordan said. "But she's not a jock."

"Exactly," Brynn said. "That's why it was so amazing."

"What do you think happened?" Jordan said. "Why did she do so well all of a sudden?"

Brynn stopped. Alyssa's explanation had been that the amethyst gave her new power—even athletic power. But Brynn obviously couldn't tell Jordan that.

"Um, vitamins," she said. "Alyssa's been taking a ton of vitamins lately."

"Interesting," Jordan said. He started typing something onto the computer. Winnie leaned close and whispered something in his ear. Brynn didn't like the looks of that whisper. What exactly was going on between them?

Jordan and Winnie stood up. "Sorry, Brynn," Jordan said. "We've got to go. We're working on a story."

"Oh?" Brynn said. "What is it?"

Jordan glanced at Winnie, who looked, to Brynn's mind, unbearably smug. "Um, I can't say. It's top secret."

"Top secret?" How annoying. He and Winnie were working on a top secret story together, which totally left Brynn out. "Good luck with that."

"Thanks," Jordan said. "See you later."

"See you," Winnie called as they left.

Brynn sat at her computer, fuming. She could hardly concentrate on story ideas now. All she could think about was Jordan and Winnie working together. Having a secret. Winnie whispering into his ear.

Jordan had been friendly enough toward her, but he hadn't exactly sought her out since they got to camp. Brynn couldn't tell from his behavior how he felt about her. And what about Winnie? Maybe Jordan liked *her* now. It was hard to say. But it sure seemed clear that Winnie liked *him*.

△ △ △

Alyssa sat in the sun, in a swirl of noise and confusion. She was surrounded by her friends from camp, and crowded around them was a huge throng of thousands of people, yelling and cheering. She smelled food, a roasting smell, hot dogs, popcorn, peanuts . . . There they all were, all her bunkmates: Natalie, Brynn, Chelsea, Alex, Jenna, Gaby, Tori, Priya, Valerie, Candace, Sloan, even Mandy. Their faces were blurred, but she knew they were there.

Suddenly, something small and hard and white flew at them out of nowhere. What was it? A small bird? A tiny angel? Alyssa shielded her face and ducked, but the hard white thing hit Chelsea smack in the head and knocked her over. Somebody screamed. Everyone crowded around Chelsea. The world went dark. Then, in the darkness, Alyssa saw a flashing red light. Chelsea's eyes were closed, but red light pulsed over her face like the lights of an ambulance. Chelsea was taken away. Two doors slammed shut. The red lights flashed, and then everything went black.

Something was wrong. Something was terribly wrong . . .

△ △ △

"Aaah!" Alyssa shouted and sat up. Her eyes flew open. She looked around.

Morning sun poured in through the window next to her bunk. All around her, she heard the soft breathing of her bunkmates. Oh. She was at camp. She'd been dreaming.

"What's the matter?" Mandy asked from her bed.

"I had a bad dream," Alyssa said. She reached under her pillow for Amy the amethyst. The other girls began to wake up.

"Are you okay?" Mandy asked.

"I will be," Alyssa said. "As soon as I figure out what my dream meant."

Mandy got up and bustled around the cabin, getting dressed. "I've got a counselor's meeting in the lodge before breakfast," she said. "So I might be a little late. I'll meet you girls in the mess hall, okay?"

"Okay," someone said. Alyssa didn't know who had spoken; she wasn't paying attention. She was too busy trying to read the signals she picked up while rubbing the amethyst.

The minutes flew by. Alyssa hardly noticed the time. Natalie shook her knee and said, "Alyssa? You coming to breakfast?"

Alyssa opened her eyes. "I'll be right there."

The other girls left for the mess hall. Alyssa dressed quickly, stashed Amy away in her hiding spot, and ran up the path to meet them.

"What was all that moaning about this morning?" Jenna asked over scrambled eggs.

"It sounded like someone was stuffing socks into your mouth," Gaby said. "And finally you couldn't take it anymore and screamed."

"I had a dream," Alyssa said. "A prophetic dream. A bad dream."

The other girls stopped mid-bite. "About us?" Candace asked.

"What happened?" Sloan asked.

"We were somewhere outdoors," Alyssa said. "We were all there, everyone in the bunk. Everything was okay until suddenly this white . . . thing . . . roared out of nowhere and conked Chelsea on the head."

Chelsea's hand flew to her forehead. "*My* head? What kind of white thing?"

"I couldn't really see it," Alyssa said. "Everything happened so fast. But after that you closed your eyes, and you never opened them again."

Everyone gasped. Chelsea looked horrified. "Did she die?" Brynn asked.

"I don't know," Alyssa said. "It wasn't clear. But I think she was hurt. Because then I saw these throbbing red lights, like ambulance lights—"

"Oh my gosh!" Chelsea cried.

"What does it mean?" Natalie asked.

"I'm not sure," Alyssa said. "But I have a feeling the answer will come eventually, in some form or another. I just hope I'll know it when I see it."

"So something bad is going to happen to me?" Chelsea said. "You're just not sure what it is yet? But I might get conked in the head?"

"I don't know for sure, Chelsea," Alyssa said.

"Maybe getting hit in the head was just a symbol," Natalie said. "Maybe it stands for something else—something less . . . painful."

Chelsea frowned and pushed her plate away, her eggs uneaten. "I don't like this one bit. I don't believe in all your silly rock magic, and I don't like being dreamed about without my permission!"

"Sorry, Chelsea," Alyssa said. "I'll ask you to sign a waiver next time."

"I think Alyssa's dream was a premonition," Sloan said. "A prediction of something that's going to happen."

"What?" Chelsea said. "I'm going to be killed by a mysterious white thing? You're saying that's really going to happen?"

"That's crazy," Alex said. "Alyssa can't predict the future in her dreams."

"Of course she can," Gaby said. "Haven't you been paying attention? How do you explain all the weird things that she's been able to do since she found Amanda?"

"That's Amy," Alyssa said.

"I would have named her Amanda," Gaby said. "If it were up to me."

"Well it isn't up to you." Alyssa was annoyed.

"How about, um, coincidence?" Tori said.

"What about Tumtum?" Natalie said. "Alyssa interpreted my dream completely right. Like she read my mind. And she predicted the correct outcome."

"Oh, like that was so hard to figure out," Chelsea said.

The 6B table was divided on the issue. Natalie, Sloan, Brynn, Gaby, and Valerie believed that Amy had given Alyssa some kind of psychic power. Alex, Jenna, Chelsea, Priya, Tori, and Candace thought it was all a bunch of hogwash.

Mandy arrived fresh from her counselors' meeting. "Big news, girls!" She paused and looked at the flushed, irritated faces at her table. "Now what's the matter?"

"Nothing," Alyssa said. "What's the big news?"

"We're going on a surprise field trip!" Mandy said. "In a couple of weeks. Dr. Steve just finalized the details."

"Where?" Tori asked.

"To Philadelphia," Mandy said. "To a baseball game! Mets versus Phillies. The whole camp is going."

"Excellent!" Valerie and Gaby, who were both from Philadelphia and big Phillies fans, high-fived each other.

"Yes!" Chelsea cheered. She was from Pennsylvania, too.

Natalie nudged Alyssa. "Go Mets!"

"My psychic prediction: The Mets are going down!" Alyssa was psyched. Her hometown in South Jersey was practically a suburb of Philadelphia, and she'd been a Phillies fan all her life. Nat wasn't a big baseball fan, but she'd be sure to root for the New York Mets.

But then, there in the stuffy mess hall amid all the excitement, Alyssa suddenly shivered. A baseball game. Of course. That was it! The key to everything!

"Wait," she said. "We can't go."

"What?" Everyone at the table stopped celebrating and stared at her. "What are you talking about?" Gaby said.

"My dream," Alyssa said. "This explains everything. That white thing I saw flying at Chelsea's head was a baseball!"

"Oh, Alyssa," Mandy said. "Don't you think you're taking this dream interpretation a little too far?"

"But I have such a strong feeling about this," Alyssa said. "If we go to that game, Chelsea will get hit in the head by a foul ball. She'll probably be seriously hurt. Flashing red lights? *Ambulance?*"

"We can't go?" Priya said. "Are you sure?"

Alyssa nodded. "Very sure."

"But—I want to go on the field trip," Chelsea whined.

"You'll be taking a big risk if you do," Alyssa said.

"I don't believe this," Tori said.

"Has the amethyst ever steered us wrong?" Sloan said.

Everyone grew quiet. No one could deny that Amy the amethyst had an amazing record. Five straight predictions in a row.

Chelsea frowned. "I guess I should listen to Alyssa, just to be on the safe side."

"I won't go, either," Sloan said. "I don't dare defy the all-seeing wisdom of Amy."

"Do any of you want to go?" Mandy asked.

Gaby raised her hand, but Chelsea knocked it down. No one else moved.

"None of you?" Mandy said. "You all believe Alyssa's dream will come true?"

No one said a word.

Mandy sighed. "Well, I'll have to clear this with Dr. Steve, but if none of you go, then I can't go. We'll all stay here and weed the vegetable garden or something *thrilling* like that."

"Ohh," the girls groaned. Even Alyssa had to admit that staying behind—even without the weeding—wasn't as much fun as a real Major League baseball game.

"I know," Mandy said. "Dullsville. Well, the game is still a ways away. You have time to change your minds. I hope you'll all come to your senses. But if you don't, so be it. It's your decision."

Breakfast was over. It was time for morning swim. Hardly anyone had finished her eggs. They all stared at Alyssa as they got up from the table. Some of them gazed at her in awe. Others glared in annoyance.

"All I can say is, you better be right about this," Chelsea said.

"I am," Alyssa said. She was sure of it.

chapter SEVEN

The Lakeview Tattler

Bunk Roundup

by Jordan

Here at *The Lakeview Tattler*, we like to know what's going on, and you can trust us to fill you in, day by day, bunk by bunk!

First division: The intrepid boys of bunk 1D are learning to swim, and their coach tells me that by the end of the summer they'll all have the crawl down perfectly. Some of the first-division girls are making a giant daisy chain to surprise their beloved counselor, Anita.

Whoops! Guess I just spilled the beans. Sorry, girls! (Just kidding. They told me it was okay to spread the news. Anyone with extra daisies to spare—or any flower at all, even clover—is asked to contribute it to the girls' cause. They're running low. Just drop off your flowers at bunk 1C.)

Bunk 3B is planning to raid bunk 3C for candy and good comic books. Keep your eyes open, 3C!

The fifth-division girls have asked me to report that they are simultaneously the coolest and the hottest girls at camp this year, and all the other girls can go jump off the pier. So there! And bunk 6B: Watch your backs. 5C wants revenge for the obstacle course debacle. The swim relay was postponed, but they want you to reschedule, if you're brave enough to take them on. They're coming for you! And this time they want to make it interesting. The girls of 5C propose a bet: The team that loses the swim relay has to go to the Midsummer Dance in their swimsuits! An anonymous resident of 5C says, "We can't wait to see those 6B girls dancing under the stars in their bathing suits! And we're sure the rest of camp will think it's funny, too." We'll see.

In sixth-division news, my sources tell me there's nothing to report. However, my colleagues here at *The Lakeview Tattler* think they're hiding something. I've asked just about every girl in bunk 6B for news, and they all clam up like, well, clams. Surely there must be something happening in a bunk full of dynamic girls. Give it up, bunk 6B. What's your secret?

And campwide, the big news is the surprise bonus field trip to the Mets-Phillies game. Everybody's talking about it, everybody's very excited. Way awesome! Thanks, Dr. Steve! Who loves ya, baby?

Got news? How about juicy gossip?

We're not picky! Tell it to us here at the newspaper office or—if you prefer to remain anonymous—drop us a note. Anything from arts and crafts projects to sports achievements to deadly vendettas welcome.

"What a waste of paper," Natalie said. She sat on the cool front porch of the lodge, reading the latest edition of *The Lakeview Tattler*. She tossed the paper in a recycling bin.

"I don't know about that." Donovan, who Nat couldn't help noticing was sitting at the other end of the long wooden bench, folded up his own copy of the paper. "You're in bunk 6B, aren't you? What's the deal? Are you all hiding something?"

Natalie, a terrible liar, immediately got nervous, and she knew it showed on her face. "What? No. What could we be hiding?"

Don't mention the amethyst. Don't mention the amethyst, she reminded herself. She believed in Amy's powers almost as much as Alyssa did. And the last thing she needed was to be cursed for life because she broke a superswear.

"Well, something's up," Donovan said. "I know a few of your bunkmates, and if you ask me, you're all giving off weird vibes. Not that I mind."

Natalie smiled and relaxed a bit. Was Donovan flirting with her? "My name's Natalie, by the way."

"Donovan," he said. As if she didn't know. He fanned the folded newspaper in front of his face. "It's so hot this summer. My bunk is an oven."

"Ours is hot, too," Natalie said. "I thought it would be cooler here on the porch, but it's not that cool."

"Maybe we'll *all* wish we could go to the dance in our bathing suits," Donovan said. "If it stays this hot."

Natalie smirked. "We're going to win that relay. The 5C girls will be dancing in their swimsuits, not us."

"As long as somebody's wearing bathing suits, I'll be happy," Donovan joked.

An awkward silence settled over them as Natalie tried desperately to think of something else to say. This was the first time she'd gotten so close to Donovan, and she hadn't expected to feel so flustered around him.

"You know where it's a *lot* cooler?" Donovan said. "Out on the lake."

Aha—an opening. *Thank you, Donovan.*

"I bet it is," Natalie said. "Wouldn't it be nice to go for a sail?"

"That's a great idea," Donovan said. "I'm pretty sure Hank's still down at the dock, and I bet he'd let us use one of the boats. Let's go for a sunset sail."

Natalie knew that she'd basically put this idea into Donovan's head herself, but now that he'd officially asked her to sail with him, she hesitated. She was still unsure what was going on with Logan, but part of her hoped they'd get back together, at least for the summer. Still, he hadn't exactly sought her out. In fact, she'd hardly seen him since the cookout. Once she saw him playing tetherball with his bunk of little kids, but when she called to him, he didn't answer. She wasn't sure if he hadn't heard her or if he was ignoring her for some reason.

"It's really beautiful out on the water this time of day," Donovan said.

Why not? She didn't owe Logan anything. And it was just a sail. No big deal.

"Sure," Nat said. "I'd love it."

Donovan tramped down the path to the lake, Natalie beside him in her flip-flops. The camp was quiet, most of the campers resting before dinner. It was a hot afternoon, but clear and beautiful. The lake was calm—smooth and glassy. Just as Donovan had predicted, Hank, the sailing instructor, was busy repairing a torn sail.

"Hey, Hank," Donovan said. "Is it okay if we take a boat out for a spin?"

"Sure," Hank said. "I'll keep an eye on you. Don't stay out too long, though."

"We won't." Donovan led Nat to a Sunfish tied to the dock. "Hop aboard," he said. She climbed on while he untied the dock rope. Then he set up the sails and in a few minutes the light breeze took them out onto the lake.

"It really is cooler out here," Natalie said.

"Told you," Donovan said. "Look out there."

Across the lake, to the west, the sun burned low through the pine trees. It glowed orange on the deep green water.

"It's beautiful," Nat said. "This is so relaxing."

"I love sailing," Donovan said. "No matter what's bothering me on dry land, I forget all about it when I'm on the water. Unless the thing that's bothering me is in the boat with me."

"What do you mean?" Natalie knew that Gaby was Donovan's sailing partner. Was he saying she got on his nerves? Not that Nat blamed him.

"It's just, you know, I can lose my temper when I'm racing," Donovan said. "And if my crew's not doing her job, I get ticked off."

Yep, it was Gaby all right. Nat had a feeling Gaby was a very inept sailor. But she respected Donovan for not naming names.

Donovan tacked, and the boat turned and glided across the water in the other direction. Now Natalie faced the dock. She thought she saw someone out there, standing on the end of the dock. The boat sailed closer, and the image became clearer. There was definitely someone standing there, and it wasn't Hank. It was a boy. A boy with binoculars. A boy watching their boat through binoculars. Weird.

"Ready to go in?" Donovan said. "It's almost dinnertime."

"I'm ready," Nat said. "This sure was nice."

"We should go for a moonlight sail soon," Donovan said. "That's even nicer."

Ooh, romantic, Nat thought. This Donovan guy sure knew how to make a girl swoon.

As they pulled closer to the dock, Nat got a better look at the boy with the binoculars. It was Logan!

What was he doing? Why was he watching her—with binoculars? Was he spying on her?

"What's this dude's problem?" Donovan said. He'd noticed Logan, too. Logan backed away as the boat skimmed up to the dock. But he hovered nearby, as if waiting to talk to Natalie, or to see who she was with.

Donovan tied the boat to the dock. Natalie, carrying her flip-flops, stepped off the boat onto the rough boards. Logan stepped forward. He seemed to want to talk to her.

"Hey," she said. "What are you doing here? Ow!" A pinprick of pain shot through her big toe. "Rats! I think I stepped on a splinter," she said. She looked up at Logan, expecting him to come help her, or at least ask if she was okay. Instead, he went pale, as if he'd seen a ghost, and without a word he ran off.

What a jerk, she thought. He didn't even offer to help her!

"Are you all right?" Donovan said. Natalie sat on the dock. Donovan took her foot in his hands and looked for the splinter. Now *that* was how a boy should behave.

"It's in my big toe," she told him.

"I see it." Donovan pinched his fingernails together and plucked out the splinter. "Got it." He showed her the tiny bit of wood. "Better?"

"Thanks." Nat was careful to put her flip-flops on before she stood up. "And thanks again for the sail."

"Any time," Donovan said.

They walked together to the mess hall, where

they split up to sit with their bunks. Gaby glared at Nat when she saw her walk in with Donovan. Across the room, Nat spotted Logan, but his back was to the door and he didn't see her.

What's his problem? she wondered. Why was he acting so strangely, watching her, then running away like that? It had to mean something, but what?

△ △ △

"Did you see Donovan and Natalie tonight?" Chelsea asked Gaby. They were sitting on the lodge porch after dinner, eating Popsicles and hoping the night would cool off before bed. "They walked into the mess hall together."

"How could I miss it?" Gaby said. Donovan had been wearing his boating shoes. Conclusion: He must have taken Natalie sailing. The conclusion was confirmed when Natalie had sat down at the sixth-division table and Alyssa had said, "What happened to you? I looked for you on the lodge porch, but you weren't there."

"I went for a sunset sail," Natalie had said. She didn't say more, though she looked as if she had plenty more to say. Obviously she'd fill Alyssa in on all the details later. The whole scene made Gaby queasy.

Since Natalie had apparently found Donovan on the porch earlier that day, Gaby decided to park there for the evening and see if he showed up again. No such luck.

"Why her?" she said to Chelsea. "Why Natalie? Why Priya? Why not me?"

"Why not *you?*" Chelsea said. "Why not *me?*

What have I done wrong? I haven't made a complete fool of myself in front of him like you have."

"Hey." Gaby resented that. "Getting knocked into the water is a rite of passage in sailing. Candace told me. It happens to everyone."

"It's hard to get him alone," Chelsea said. "There always seems to be at least one girl hovering around."

"I keep trying to get his attention," Gaby said. "And it keeps backfiring. I'm not giving up, though. I want Donovan to fall for me like a klutz on ice skates. Like he's never fallen for anyone before."

Chelsea laughed. "Good luck with *that*. You've got a lot of competition. Though the klutz part sounds right."

"I have a new plan," Gaby said. "I may not be able to get his attention with my sailing ability—"

"Since you don't have any," Chelsea said.

Gaby flashed her an annoyed look, but ignored the snarky comment since it was, technically, the truth. "I'll get his attention by doing what I do best."

"And what, exactly, is that?"

"I thought about it long and hard," Gaby said. "And the thing I do best in the whole wide world is make chocolate peanut butter Rice Krispies treats."

"What an astounding talent," Chelsea said. "That ought to blow his socks off."

"Well, boys like to eat," Gaby said. "The way to the heart is through the stomach, and all that. It's worth a try."

"I think I'll just walk around looking cool and beautiful and haughty until he must have me," Chelsea said.

Chelsea had always been cool and beautiful and haughty, but as far as Gaby knew, she'd never had a boyfriend. "How is that different from what you usually do?"

"It's not," Chelsea said. "But it's got to work someday."

"It won't work on Donovan," Gaby said.

"Why not?" Chelsea said.

"Because it has nothing to do with love," Gaby said.

"Love?" Chelsea laughed. "Keep dreaming."

▲ ▲ ▲

"Are you going to enter the nature fair?" Gwenda asked Alyssa. They were leaving the nature shack after a particularly fraught session in which Roseanne showed them which local plants were safe to nibble on and which were poisonous. Somehow Gwenda had brought up the subject of plants' use in medicine. Alyssa said they were often used in potions and spells, especially to attract love or to curse an enemy. Gwenda countered that unlike medicinal cures, none of Alyssa's superstitions had ever been proven. Alyssa said they weren't superstitions, they were folk remedies. The two of them argued until Roseanne pointed out that both girls were basically talking about the same thing: using plants to solve problems.

And now Gwenda was asking about the nature fair? Alyssa's guard was up. Gwenda struck her as the competitive grade-grubbing type, desperate to win contests and score extra points. Sort of the way Brynn described Candace, except that Candace was actually nice. *And* Candace was open-minded enough to put some faith into "superstitions" like the amethyst.

Instead of answering Gwenda's question, Alyssa countered with a question of her own. "Are *you* entering the nature fair?"

"Definitely," Gwenda said. "I've been planning my project since before I left for camp. What are you working on?"

Alyssa wasn't really working on anything. In the back of her mind she considered writing up a report about the amethyst's power and the outcome of all the predictions she'd made since she'd found it. But that would mean revealing its existence, and she wasn't ready to do that yet. "Do we have to do a project, or is it optional?" she asked.

Gwenda shrugged. "I think it's optional. But you should do a project. You seem very interested in nature. You get very emotional about it."

"Emotional?" Alyssa said. "What's that supposed to mean?"

"Just that you need to see your feelings reflected in nature," Gwenda said. "You want to find magic there, so you twist the facts around until you make them look magical."

"What?" Alyssa's face flamed red. What was it about Gwenda that set her off so much? "You're the one who won't see the truth. You discount any facts that don't fit what you think of as science. You only believe in things that you can prove, but you won't make room in your theory for mystery. The universe is full of things you can't explain. But just because you can't explain them doesn't mean they don't exist!"

"Your highly emotional response to this subject is keeping you from thinking clearly," Gwenda said.

"Your highly unemotional response to everything means you're missing out on the beauty of nature!" Alyssa said.

"Beauty is subjective," Gwenda said. "It's not a fact."

"It is so a fact!" Alyssa hardly knew what she was saying, she was so mad. People like Gwenda missed the whole point of everything—to see the world, absorb it, enjoy it, and stop thinking about it so much. "Beauty is a fact. Look." Alyssa pointed at the sky, which was the clear, soft blue of a fine china teacup. "Look at that sky. The color. Isn't that beautiful?"

"I think it's beautiful," Gwenda said. "But that's only my opinion. The fact is, that color is caused by the ozone and high pressure in the atmosphere, and—"

"But anybody on earth looking at that sky would say it is beautiful," Alyssa said. "Doesn't that make it true? If everyone in the whole world agrees that it's true?"

"Not necessarily," Gwenda said. "I have no way of knowing what everyone in the world thinks about that color. Until you provide evidence, I cannot accept your statement as fact."

Alyssa sighed with frustration. "You're missing the point! I give up. There's no use arguing with you," she said, and ran off to the arts and crafts room. *I think I'll make a voodoo doll*, she thought. *And it's going to look a lot like Gwenda.*

That afternoon, Gaby went into the kitchen during a free period. The cook was busy chopping vegetables, but he agreed to let Gaby use the equipment she needed to make a pan of chocolate peanut butter Rice Krispies treats. Rice Krispies, marshmallows, chocolate chips, peanut butter . . . She had to admit that they weren't exactly hard to make, though her father always said hers were the best. She had the magic touch, that's what he said. Ever since Alyssa had found that amethyst, Gaby was beginning to believe in magic more and more. If Amy worked magic for Alyssa, maybe Rice Krispies treats would work magic for Gaby. Stranger things had happened. Especially in the past few days.

When the bars were done, Gaby let them cool, then cut them into neat, generous squares. She wrapped them in aluminum foil and tied the package with a red ribbon. There. At the very least, Donovan's bunkmates would be jealous.

After dinner, everyone met for a campfire sing-along under the stars. Gaby found Donovan sitting with his friends on a log near the fire. She walked over to them, carrying her package of treats.

"Hi, Donovan," she said.

"Hey there, first mate," he said. They'd had another disastrous day of sailing that morning—tangled ropes, improperly tied knots coming loose, sails falling into the water, general chaos—but Donovan never seemed to hold it against her. She thought he might ask to be switched with another partner, but so far he just laughed at her utter incompetence, as if it amused him. But not in a good way. It seemed to amuse him the way slapstick clowns are funny, not the way girls you have a crush on are endearing. Gaby was determined to change that.

"I brought you something." Gaby offered him the tinfoil-wrapped package. "To make up for the mess I made this morning."

"Dude, thanks." He took the package and opened it up. He stared at the squares in the darkness. It was hard to see much in the firelight. "What is it?"

"Dessert," Gaby said. "The stewed prunes they served after dinner tonight are not what I'd call a treat."

Donovan laughed. "Me neither." He picked up one of the Rice Krispies treats and sniffed it, then immediately dropped it. "Sorry, dudette, but do these have peanuts in them?"

Rats. She knew what was coming. "Peanut butter," she said.

"Totally allergic," Donovan said, pointing to himself. "One bite could send me to the emergency room. Actually, I shouldn't even be touching them." He offered the bars to his friends. "Any of you guys want these?"

"I'm allergic, too, dude," one of Donovan's friends said.

"I hate the smell of peanut butter," another one said.

"I'll eat them." A third boy grabbed the package and started stuffing Rice Krispies treats into his mouth.

"Sorry about that," Gaby said. "I didn't know."

"No worries," Donovan said. "Nice try, Gaby. Thanks for the thought. See you on deck tomorrow—and this time, don't wear red-soled sneakers. They leave marks on the boat."

"Good to know," Gaby said, feeling dejected. "Thanks for the tip."

"Any time. Dudes, do you know this one?"

Donovan and his friends started singing some emo song Gaby didn't know, with Donovan on air guitar. She walked away. Another failure.

What did it take to win him over? Gaby was stumped. She needed help. Huge help. Supernatural help.

▲ ▲ ▲

"Alyssa, please," Gaby begged. She'd cornered Alyssa in the bunk after lunch the next day. "I'm desperate."

"I'm sure you are," Alyssa said. She stroked Amy as if the amethyst were a pet mouse. For some reason Gaby found the gesture annoying. "But I don't want to misuse Amy. You heard what Sloan said. It could come back to bite us in the butt—karma-wise, I mean."

"Just ask it again who Donovan is taking to the dance," Gaby said. In her mind, the dance was the big event of the summer, the night when couples would be made or broken. "Maybe the situation has changed a little. After all, he's been seen canoodling with a lot of girls, but not with Candace."

"Oh, all right." Alyssa closed her eyes and held Amy tight. "Who will Donovan ask to the dance?" she murmured like an incantation. "Donovan . . .

dance . . . Donovan . . . dance . . ."

Gaby waited nervously, biting her fingernails. "Also, if you see any hints for what I can do that he'd actually appreciate—things that don't threaten his life like Rice Krispies treats—that would help."

"Okay, but don't break my concentration," Alyssa said.

Gaby sat back to leave Alyssa to her psychic work. Alyssa had gotten a little full of herself since she'd become an all-seeing goddess of the supernatural, Gaby thought.

Alyssa opened her eyes. "Sorry, Gaby," she said. "I looked and looked, but all I see is Candace."

"Rats." Gaby frowned.

"Don't be sad," Alyssa said. "I'm not infallible. I could be wrong." Gaby braced herself for the sentence she knew was coming next. "Of course, I haven't been wrong yet. But there's always a first time."

Natalie popped into the cabin. "Alyssa, come on. You'll be late for your makeover."

"Coming. Sorry, I have to go," Alyssa said to Gaby.

"You're getting a makeover?" Gaby said. "With Yvette?" Yvette was a counselor who was also a makeup pro. Everyone wanted a makeover from her, but she'd only give them under special circumstances.

"She won it for shredding the obstacle course, remember?" Natalie said.

"I'm not really into makeup," Alyssa said with a shrug. "But it's free, so why not, right?"

"Yeah," Gaby muttered. "Why not?" Everything was going Alyssa's way lately. "You know, maybe some good things would happen to me if *I* had a lucky amethyst."

"Maybe," Alyssa said. "But it helps if you've got the gift in the first place."

"Right," Gaby said. "The gift." As far as she could tell, the only gift Alyssa had was Amy. "What if I borrowed Amy for a few hours?" she said. "Maybe some of her good fortune would rub off on me. Maybe I'd even develop psychic powers of my own."

Alyssa put Amy in her pocket and patted her protectively. "Sorry, Gaby, I can't."

"Why not?"

"I just don't want anything to happen to her," Alyssa said.

"I promise to take good care of her," Gaby said. "Please, Alyssa? Just for one hour."

"I can't," Alyssa said. "The amethyst is too powerful. I can't let her get into the wrong hands."

"The wrong hands?" This comment was extra super-duper annoying. What was wrong with Gaby's hands? Why were they any more wrong than Alyssa's? It wasn't like she would lose the amethyst or anything.

"I've got to go." Alyssa left, taking Amy with her.

She thinks she's so great, Gaby thought. *But she'd be nothing without that rock.*

Gaby knew Alyssa usually hid the amethyst before she left the bunk, and she wouldn't tell anyone where—not even Natalie. But this time she took the stone with her—probably because she was afraid to hide Amy with Gaby lurking around.

Amy is the key, Gaby thought. The key to finding a way to Donovan's crush center, if not his actual heart. *If only I could get my hands on it, just for a little while . . .*

An evil plan began to take shape in her mind. Well, not all that evil. Alyssa had *found* the amethyst on the ground at camp. It's not like she *bought* it or anything. She didn't own it, which meant she should be willing to share.

Tonight, Gaby thought, *when everyone leaves for dinner, I'll hide and wait and see where Alyssa hides Amy. Then, when I get a chance, I'll just borrow the stone for a few minutes. I've got to feel her power for myself.*

When I'm finished soaking up Amy's incredible power, I'll put her back. No harm done.

Gaby couldn't think of a single reason why she shouldn't do this. After all, why should Alyssa have all the mystical power? It wasn't fair. Gaby was just evening things out a little.

Later that day, just before dinner, Gaby put stage one of her plan into effect. Mandy herded all the 6B girls off to the mess hall. As usual, Alyssa lingered, saying she'd catch up. Gaby left, trying to look innocent and inconspicuous.

But she hung back as the group walked up the path toward the mess hall. Then she slipped off the path and hid behind a tree. No one noticed. At least, she didn't think so. Mandy would reprimand her—and Alyssa—for not staying with the group, but this was worth a little scolding.

She doubled back down the path to the cabin. When she got close, she crept though the woods, darting from tree to bush to shrub, hoping she wouldn't be seen.

She hid behind a large bush just outside the bunk. From there, she could see Alyssa through a cabin window. The window next to Alyssa's bed opened slightly. Alyssa's hand reached out, holding something that had to be Amy. The hand dropped the stone in a small niche behind the shutters, on the cabin's outside wall.

So, she hides Amy outside, Gaby thought. *Very clever, Alyssa. Very clever.*

Gaby had the information she needed. She hurried up the path to the mess hall before anyone missed her, and before Alyssa spotted her. She'd put stage two into effect later. Now that she knew Amy's hiding place, she had all the time in the world.

chapter

EIGHT

"Hey, Alyssa." Valerie burst into the bunk after dinner. Heat lightning flared in the distance, so the outdoor activity was canceled. "Did you see that poster outside the mess hall?"

"Poster?" Alyssa said. "No, I didn't notice."

"It said that somebody lost an amethyst," Valerie said.

Alyssa froze. Her amethyst belonged to someone else? No! This was her worst nightmare come true. There had to be a mistake.

"Amethyst?" Alyssa said. "Are you sure? Maybe it said somebody lost an abacus."

Valerie raised her eyebrows. "An abacus? First of all, I know how to read. Second of all, who would bring an abacus to camp? Or anywhere?"

"You never know," Alyssa said. "Some of these younger kids are *really* geeky."

"The poster didn't say *abacus*," Valerie said. "I'll quote it to you if you want. It said 'Lost: Large Unpolished Amethyst. If found, please return to bunk 5C.'"

"Bunk 5C!" Now Alyssa was really nervous.

"Don't you see, Valerie? This could be a conspiracy. Or a prank! Maybe someone in 5C heard about Amy and wants to test her superpowers for herself. Did any of you tell? Did anybody break our superswear to secrecy?"

"No," Priya said.

"Not me," Candace said.

"Nobody spilled your stupid secret," Chelsea said.

"They might have overheard us talking, then," Alyssa said. "I still say this is some kind of conspiracy."

"Or maybe," Mandy said, "just maybe, somebody in 5C lost her amethyst and wants it back. Of all the possibilities, I'd say that's the most likely."

Alyssa still didn't buy it. But she had to admit it *was* possible. Mandy stood over her, hands on her hips, looking no-nonsense and practical like she always did. At that moment, Alyssa found *no-nonsense* and *practical* to be very irritating personality traits. But she knew what Mandy was waiting to hear.

"Okay," Alyssa said. "I'll find out who the amethyst belongs to. And I'll give it back tomorrow, as soon as I get a chance."

"Promise?" Mandy said.

"Promise," Alyssa said. She noticed that as she said the words, two of her fingers involuntarily crossed themselves.

🏕 🏕 🏕

"Natalie, what's wrong?" When Alyssa woke up the next morning, she found Natalie lying awake in bed, her eyes wide with fright.

"I had another weird dream," Natalie said. "It was kind of scary."

Alyssa reached under her pillow for Amy. "I'm ready," she said. "Pour out the messages sent to you from your unconscious mind. Amy and I are prepared to interpret your most secret, innermost thoughts."

Natalie hesitated. Alyssa thought she looked slightly queasy, but maybe she was just hungry for breakfast. The other girls gathered around to hear Alyssa's interpretation. It had become a morning ritual in bunk 6B.

"Do my dream next," Brynn said.

"Natalie first," Alyssa said.

"Okay," Natalie said. "Here's my dream: I was here at camp, except it was winter. The camp was deserted. No one else was here. The lake was frozen, the trees were bare, and a plastic bag blew across the path for some reason."

"Very poetic," Chelsea said.

"Then what happened?" Priya said.

"I walked into a bunk—a boys' bunk," Natalie said. "The door creaked. I brushed aside some cobwebs. The bunk was dusty, and all the mattresses were bare. Then for some reason I looked at the counselor's cot . . . and I saw Logan lying there. His face was whitish-blue, like ice. And his eyes were open, staring."

Brynn clutched Tori. "This is spooky."

Alyssa stayed calm, rubbing the stone, keeping her eyes closed and concentrating on the images in the dream.

"No talking, please," she said. "I need to get the

pure dream, directly from Natalie, with no distractions."

"Sorry," Brynn said.

"I shook his shoulder to wake him up, but his body was all stiff," Natalie said. "Logan was . . . dead!"

Brynn and Valerie shrieked. Alyssa opened her eyes.

"Poor Natalie!" Mandy said. She sat beside Natalie and patted her back. "What a terrible dream. Are you all right?"

Natalie nodded. "I think so. But what does it mean? It's not a premonition of some kind, is it, Alyssa?"

Alyssa closed her eyes again and ran Natalie's dream images through her mind like a movie. It was such a scary dream—but unlike the other girls, Alyssa didn't pick up scary vibes from it, which seemed strange. She didn't want to lead Natalie in the wrong direction, so she thought it over carefully. Did Natalie's dream predict the future? Was Logan in danger?

Alyssa didn't sense any danger, so she opened her eyes and smiled, calm as a Buddha. "Don't worry, Natalie, your dream is not a premonition. My new age book says dreams don't usually predict the future. They're more like a snapshot of your soul."

"A snapshot of your soul?" Candace said.

"What in the world does *that* mean?" Natalie asked. "That I want Logan dead?"

"Of course not," Alyssa said. "Your dream doesn't mean that *Logan* is dying—it means your *feelings* for him are dying. It's kind of symbolic. Ever since you got to camp, you've been wondering if you want to get back together with Logan, right? So now your dream is giving you the answer. It's telling you what you want, even if you don't know it yet."

Sitting on her bed, Natalie leaned forward and rested her elbows on her knees. "So what do I want?" she asked.

Alyssa reached for a bottle of water she kept near her bed. "Well, I guess you don't want to get back with him. Your feelings for him are dying."

"Feelings are dying," Candace echoed. "That doesn't really sound like Natalie."

Alyssa held up Amy as if that was all she needed to silence the unbelievers.

"But . . . I'm not sure my feelings for him *are* dying," Natalie said. "He's been acting weird lately—very weird. But I was kind of thinking I still liked him, if he'd just stay still for a second and stop running away from me."

"According to Amy, you're getting over him," Alyssa said. "It's a good thing. You're ready to move on to something better, more mature."

"You sound like my mother's therapist," Tori said.

"Now do me," Sloan said. "I'm sleeping, and my mother comes into my room and wakes me up. She says she's really an alien queen, and when I say I don't believe her, she rips off her head! And underneath is this pulsing green blob! She really *is* an alien queen. By the way, did I wake up screaming this morning?"

"I didn't hear anything," Tori said.

"Alyssa, what does it mean?"

"Um . . ." Alyssa wasn't getting a clear signal from Amy about Sloan's dream. Maybe her psychic center was getting tired and needed food. Or maybe Sloan's dream was just too weird.

"It means you're mother is trying to tell you something," she said.

"But what is she trying to tell me?" Sloan said.

"That she's an alien?" Alyssa said.

"Good call," Chelsea said. "You really saw right through the symbolism of that one, Alyssa."

"Girls, we're late for breakfast." Mandy had been getting dressed while the girls described their dreams. No one else was ready to go. "We're *always* late for breakfast. Let's get a move on!"

Everyone dressed quickly. Alyssa took her time. She needed to be the last one out. As soon as everyone left, she stashed Amy in her secret nook. Then she started up the path to the mess hall. Mandy met her at the mess hall door.

"Alyssa, you've been lagging behind the group a lot lately," Mandy said. "Please try to keep up with the rest of us. I worry if someone's missing."

"I'm sorry," Alyssa said, not meeting her eyes. "I'm a slow dresser."

"Did you bring the amethyst with you?" Mandy asked.

"Whoops," Alyssa said. "I forgot." And she really had forgotten about returning it. But it was too late to get Amy now. "I thought I'd find out who the owner is first and talk to her, to make sure it's the same amethyst."

"All right," Mandy said. She started for their table. "But don't put it off."

"I'll find the owner after breakfast," Alyssa said.

"Okay," Mandy said.

But Alyssa had a swim meet after breakfast, and then arts and crafts, and she got so caught up in weaving a new straw shoulder bag as a gift for Natalie that she forgot all about Amy. Or rather, she forgot to find out who the owner was. By the time she remembered, dinner was over and everyone was gathering near the fire pit for a campfire. Too late to do anything about it then.

I'll do it tomorrow, she thought. *Whoever wants Amy back can wait one more day.*

🛖 🛖 🛖

Gaby sat around the campfire, singing her heart out, waiting for Alyssa to show up. At last Alyssa arrived, armed with marshmallows and several pointed sticks to roast them on. She passed the sticks to the girls sitting around her.

"Whoo!" Alyssa said, pushing her hair out of her face. "It's really getting windy!"

"I'll go look for more sticks," Gaby said to no one in particular. She probably didn't need to say anything; no one was paying much attention to her. Everyone was belting out the camp song.

Gaby crept away from the fire and disappeared into the shadows. Time to make her move. The stars were perfectly aligned to put her plan into effect, she thought. Not that she knew anything about stars. It didn't really matter, because when she glanced up at the sky, she couldn't see the stars. The night had gotten cloudy. Another strong gust of wind nearly pushed her over.

Once she was well away from the campfire, she turned on her flashlight. She groped her way along the path to the bunks. It was a dark night, and the whole camp was at the fire pit. No one would be in bunk 6B. No one would see what she was up to.

She had considered telling Alyssa the dream she'd had that morning, but decided not to in the end. In the dream, Gaby met a man in a red cape near the dock. A heavy mist floated over the lake. The man held out his hand, and she gave him the amethyst. In return, he opened his cape and out stepped Donovan, like a prize. The man in the cape laughed devilishly and disappeared in a puff of smoke.

Gaby was glad she'd resisted the temptation to tell her dream. Who knows, after hearing a dream like that, Alyssa might have guessed that Gaby was up to no good. Some of the other girls in the bunk might have gotten suspicious, too.

The coast was clear. The wind whipped up again, knocking a branch off a tree and carrying a metallic smell that Gaby knew meant rain was coming soon. She'd have to hurry. In the distance, she heard the voices of the other campers, boys and girls, little and big, singing a happy camp song. They sounded so innocent. Gaby felt a pang of guilt, but it was only a tiny pinprick-sized pang. What she was about to do wasn't *wrong*, exactly. Alyssa would be mad if she knew about it, but that didn't mean Gaby was a criminal or anything.

Gaby burst into the cabin. At first she didn't turn on the light, because she didn't want anyone to see her. She was just going to grab the amethyst and go.

She shined her flashlight on Alyssa's bunk. Something was wrong. Alyssa's bed was unmade, and something strange dangled from the wall in front of it.

What *was* that? It looked like a string of flags. Gaby pointed her flashlight at it and stepped closer. Hey—those weren't flags. They were panties. *Her* panties!

She tripped over something. All their shoes had been piled on the floor in a pyramid. What was going on?

No time to worry about secrecy now. Gaby needed to see. She switched on the overhead light and gasped.

The room looked as if it had been ransacked by a bear. Clothes hung out of the cubbies in disarray. All the girls' panties were strung across the room like party streamers. The beds were mussed; sneakers and flip-flops had been tossed all over the place. Two bottles of Tori's nail polish lay broken and bleeding pink and orange on the floor near her bed.

Gaby stepped toward the bathroom, afraid to look. *Oh, no.* The toilet was draped in an elaborate web of toilet paper. And on the mirror, in Chelsea's favorite magenta lip gloss, someone had scrawled, *You've been pranked!*

Amy, Gaby thought, her heart racing. Had the pranksters found the amethyst? Gaby jumped up on

Alyssa's bunk and reached out the window. She felt for the nook behind the shutter. It was empty.

Oh my god, she thought. *We've been pranked—and Amy is gone!*

chapter

NINE

Tori nudged Natalie. "There he is—Mr. Death himself."

"What are you talking about?" Natalie was roasting a marshmallow, and Tori's nudge had knocked her stick into the fire. Natalie picked it up, but the marshmallow was a flaming lost cause. "Look what you made me do." Then she glanced up and saw Logan leading his bunk around the campfire. She knew it was silly, but after the scary dream she'd had that morning, she was glad to see him alive and well. Just the sight of him made her heart beat faster. How could Alyssa say her feelings for him were dying?

"Was Alyssa right?" Tori asked. "Are your feelings for him DOA?"

"I'm not sure," Natalie said.

"Why don't you go find out?" Tori said.

"Good idea," Natalie said.

She walked over to the spot where Logan had settled his ten-year-old charges. He was leading them in a gross-out song about olives and eyeballs.

Natalie sat down on a nearby log. When the song was done, she said, "You know, olives and eyeballs really are a lot alike if you think about it."

"Totally," Logan said. But as soon as she sat down, he shifted slightly away from her, as if she had the flu and he didn't want to catch it.

The little boys went off to find roasting sticks. A group of third-division girls sat down nearby and started making their own s'mores.

"So how do you like being a CIT?" Natalie asked Logan. She knew it was a lame question, the kind of thing her mother would ask, but she didn't know what else to say. Everything had gotten so strained between them.

"It's great," Logan said. He looked away, keeping an eye on his campers. Natalie waited for him to say something else, but he didn't.

"Are they giving you any trouble?" she asked.

He shrugged. "They're a riot. They're little devils, but they can be pretty funny."

Natalie laughed. "I heard about the puke incident. So gross." One of Logan's boys had sneaked a tub of hummus from the salad bar and filled the mess hall toilet with it to make it look as if somebody had puked. The hummus clogged up the toilet and the boys' bathroom was out of order for a day and a half.

She thought Logan would laugh, but he just nodded. "Yeah, that was a disaster. Dr. Steve really chewed me out. 'You've got to learn how to keep them under control!'" He was warming up a little. Natalie could tell he liked talking about his campers. "They're just mischievous. Secretly, I find their jokes kind of entertaining. But don't tell Dr. Steve."

"I wouldn't dream of it," Natalie said, and at the word dream she shivered.

Suddenly, a little girl sitting next to Logan screamed, "Ow! OWW! Something bit me!"

Logan turned to help the girl. "Are you all right? What bit you?" She held out her leg for him to inspect, crying.

"I think it was a monster!" she wailed. "Or an alligator! It could have bitten my leg right off!"

Natalie peered over Logan's shoulder. It was hard to see in the firelight, but all she could make out was a tiny red spot on the girl's calf.

"Shhh. You're all right," Logan said. "It's just a bug bite. It might itch a little, but you won't lose your leg—I promise." He stood up. "I'll go get your counselor and have her bring over some Calamine lotion, okay?"

"Hurry up!" The girl was still crying. "It stings!"

Logan hurried away without another word. Natalie waited a few minutes to see if he'd come back. She still hadn't had a chance to find out how she felt about him. He was acting so strangely around her, it was like he wasn't even himself. She didn't know what to think. But the longer this went on, the more it bothered her.

The little girl's counselor arrived with lotion, but still no Logan. Natalie got up to return to her group. On the way she saw Logan with his boys, farther over around the circle. He'd moved them without saying anything to her.

Maybe my feelings for him should die, she thought. *It sure seems like his feelings for me are gone for good.*

▲ ▲ ▲

"Whoa," Alyssa said. "Did you feel that?" She was sitting around the campfire when a plastic marshmallow bag flew at her from nowhere, sticking to the back of her head. She peeled it off and it blew into the fire.

"I felt it," Brynn said, picking twigs from her hair.

The wind was getting stronger now, blowing sparks from the campfire. "Sorry, kids, but we're going to have to cut this short," Dr. Steve called out. "Feels like a storm coming."

A counselor dumped buckets of water on the fire to douse it. Alyssa's hair blew across her face. She could almost taste the rain in the air, an electric, mineral taste.

"Everyone back to their bunks," Dr. Steve said. "Batten down your shutters if you need to."

"All right, 6B," Mandy shouted into the wind. "Let's go."

"Hurry," Chelsea said, plucking at her navy silk peasant blouse. "This top stains my skin purple if it gets wet."

Alyssa ran ahead without waiting for the others. She couldn't help thinking of Amy in her nook outside the cabin.

"Alyssa, come back!" Mandy shouted. "Wait for the rest of us!"

Alyssa pretended she hadn't heard and kept

running. She wanted to bring the amethyst in safely before anyone saw her.

The rain started before she got to the bunk, fat hard drops pelting down on her. Alyssa ran to the outside wall of the cabin. The shutters flapped and banged in the wind. She climbed over a row of shrubs and reached behind the shutter, hoping the darkness would hide her. She pressed her hand into the little nook where she kept the amethyst.

No. Oh, no.

She felt around again. Amy wasn't there.

Then she noticed the light was on in the cabin. Someone else was in there. Alyssa ran to the purple door and went inside.

Gaby stood alone in the center of the room, staring at the mess. Cubbies had been ransacked. Panties hoisted like flags across the room, shoes all over the floor, everything a mess!

"We've been pranked!" Gaby said.

Their bunkmates, dripping and out of breath, crowded in behind Alyssa. "Holy panty raid, what happened in here?" Brynn cried.

"Somebody pranked us while we were at the campfire," Alex said.

"But who would do that?" Priya said. "Everybody at camp was there."

Mandy took over. "All right, it's no big deal," she said. "Let's get this place cleaned up."

"No big deal?" Chelsea said. "My stuff's all over the floor!" She picked up a white tank top that now had a brown dust mark across the back. "Look at this! How could someone do this to us?"

"My nail polish!" Tori cried. "Two bottles broken! My favorite colors, too."

"Is anything missing?" Natalie asked.

"Doesn't look like it," Mandy said. "It just looks like a mess."

"Something is missing," Alyssa said. "The amethyst."

Everyone gasped. "Are you sure?" Valerie asked.

"Totally," Alyssa said. "I checked my hiding place and it was gone."

"Maybe we'll find it on the floor somewhere," Alex said. Everyone started picking up their things. Alyssa looked under her pillow, among her sheets, all over the floor, in the trash can . . . no Amy.

"Did you find her?" Nat was refolding her clothes and putting them back into her cubby.

Alyssa shook her head.

"This rots," Gaby said.

When they'd cleaned up the whole cabin, Mandy called for lights out. But Alyssa couldn't sleep. No one could. Outside, the wind howled and rain beat hard on the roof.

"Who do you think pranked us?" Valerie said.

"And why?" Tori said. "What did we ever do to anybody?"

"I think it has something to do with the amethyst," Natalie said. "It must. Amy is the only thing missing."

"But no one outside this bunk knows about it," Candace said. "Do they?"

The bunk was silent for a moment. "Did

anyone tell?" Alyssa asked.

"Not me," said a voice from the dark.

"Me neither."

"No."

"No."

"I'd never—"

"Maybe someone heard about it somehow," Brynn said.

"Someone in 5C knows about Amy," Alyssa said. "Because they put up that Lost poster."

"That's right."

"Maybe someone in 5C is looking for the amethyst," Sloan said. "Maybe they decided to break into all the cabins until they found it."

"If they decided to break into all the cabins," Candace said, "they sure picked the right bunk to start with."

"We may never know what really happened," Valerie said.

"Oh, we'll find out," Chelsea said. "One way or another. We've got the whole rest of the summer to figure it out."

"I hope it doesn't take that long to get Amy back," Alyssa said. "Or our summer could be ruined."

"Alyssa, don't forget that the amethyst doesn't belong to you," Mandy said. "You were supposed to return it by now, anyway."

Oh. That's right. But Alyssa *felt* as if Amy belonged to her. Alyssa was as attached to the amethyst as she had been to her blanket when she was little. Only more so, because her blanket didn't give her psychic powers.

"Time to get some shut-eye, girls," Mandy said. "We'll work on this mystery tomorrow. Good night."

No one said another word, but Alyssa could hear her bunkmates tossing and turning and sighing sleeplessly. It was disturbing to think that someone had rifled through all their things. And taken their most valuable possession.

Alyssa obsessively went over the facts in her mind. Someone from 5C—the "real" owner of the amethyst, if that was true—might have ransacked the bunk. But Alyssa kept imagining the scene she saw when she first arrived at the bunk: Gaby, alone among the ruins.

Gaby, who had been begging Alyssa to lend her the amethyst. Who made it very clear that she wanted to try out a few psychic predictions for herself. And who was so crazy about Donovan, she'd do just about anything to win him over.

Could Gaby have stolen Amy—and made it look like a prank so no one would suspect her?

Alyssa heard Natalie in the bunk below, rolling over and fluffing her pillow. She wondered if anyone else suspected Gaby, or if she was the only one.

For now, Alyssa decided to give Gaby the benefit of the doubt. Innocent until proven guilty, and all that.

Besides, Alyssa hoped Gaby wasn't the culprit. What could be worse than having a traitor—and a thief—in your own bunk?

The Lakeview Tattler

The residents of bunk 6B returned from the campfire sing-along last night to find their cabin in a shambles. Clothes were tossed around, underwear displayed in an undignified manner, the toilet wrapped in so much toilet paper they had to hack through it with scissors before they could use it. Written on the mirror in lipstick were these words: You've been pranked.

So far there are no hard suspects in this case, though individual members of the bunk have their suspicions. Counselor Mandy reported the incident to Dr. Steve, who said he will investigate. He added that he hopes this won't inspire copycat prankings and would hate to see the summer jeopardized by a rash of unpleasant incidents. Anyone caught pulling a prank will be punished, he warned.

If you have any tips on this heinous

crime, please report them to Brynn, care of this paper. Thank you.

—Brynn

"Hey." Jordan read over Brynn's shoulder as she typed her story into the computer at the newspaper office. "Why didn't you give this story to me? I could have used it in my Bunk Roundup."

Brynn glanced around the office. It bustled with activity that morning. Jordan's friend Winnie lurked at a nearby desk. She looked as if she were thinking hard about something, but Brynn suspected Winnie was eavesdropping on her conversation with Jordan.

"I thought this was too serious a story for the Roundup," Brynn said. "More hard news than chit-chat. It is a crime story, after all."

"A crime story?" Jordan said. "Isn't that taking things kind of seriously? I mean, your bunk got messed up, but nothing was stolen or anything like that, right?"

Brynn hesitated, thinking of the amethyst. They had all agreed not to mention Amy in connection with the pranking. Alyssa thought it was best to keep the stone a secret until they figured out exactly what was going on.

"No," Brynn said. "Nothing was stolen. But still, people shouldn't be allowed to just walk into your cabin and mess up your stuff. How would *you* like it?"

Jordan raised his hands in surrender. "Of

course I wouldn't like it. Do you have any leads? Any idea who might have done it? And calm down, *I* didn't prank your bunk."

Maybe it was her imagination, but Brynn thought she saw Winnie's head lean slightly toward her, as if she were listening extra hard.

"No, we don't have any leads," Brynn said. Of course, the girls of bunk 5C were major suspects. They'd already threatened to pull a prank on 6B after they lost to them in the obstacle course. But that was a couple of weeks ago, and Brynn had assumed everyone had forgotten about it. Maybe not.

The other tie to 5C was the "lost amethyst" poster. The stone was to be returned to 5C—and now it was missing. But Brynn didn't want to mention any of this in earshot of Winnie, who, after all, was in 5C. And that meant Brynn didn't feel comfortable sharing it with Jordan, either, since he'd been spending a lot of time with Winnie, working on their "top secret" news story, whatever that was.

It was a shame, Brynn thought. She would have liked to discuss the case with Jordan. The two of them might have investigated it together. She still thought they'd make a good team.

The Lakeview Tattler

Bunk Roundup

by Jordan

First division: The nine-year-old girls in first division are suffering from a stubborn case of homesickness. To distract themselves, they're making rag dolls to send to poor children in South America. How sweet! Their counselor, Anita, reports that the project is working well.

Second division: The charitable angels of second division are making rag dolls to help the poor homesick girls of first division feel better. Now that's thoughtful.

Third division: Competition between the three boys' bunks in third division is heating up as they battle it out for their division's soccer title. Thor Gersten of bunk 3F is a superstar scorer—they say his giant head makes him uncannily accurate when he heads the ball. But 3D has killer goalie Jon Cruz on their side, and 3E's forward line is close to unbeatable. Watch the third-division soccer action every afternoon at four on the main field. Feel the heat!

Fourth and fifth divisions: Yawn! Do something interesting, you guys!

Sixth division: What's going on in 6B? There's the still-unsolved pranking, but beyond that sources report mysterious occult forces at work among the female sixth div'ers. Hard to get specifics out of anybody in that secretive crowd, but let's just say we've picked up on a seriously mystical vibe. Broomsticks flying over the night skies of Camp Lakeview? Not sure we'd go that far, but something strange is going on in that bunk, and we'd like to know more.

Got news? How about juicy gossip? We're not picky! Tell it to us here at the newspaper office or—if you prefer to remain anonymous—drop us a note. Anything from arts and crafts projects to sports achievements to deadly vendettas welcome.

"Brynn, have you been talking?" Chelsea snapped. She crumpled up the newspaper and tossed it at Brynn.

"No," Brynn said. "I haven't. I swear!" She sat with Alyssa, Chelsea, and Natalie on the dock. They had all gotten out of their electives a little early and wanted to catch some rays.

"Come on, Brynn," Natalie said. "You can tell us. Jordan's your ex, after all. Or have you guys gotten back together?"

"We haven't," Brynn said. She picked at a splinter of wood on the dock. "Not yet, anyway."

"Well, what's going on?" Alyssa said. "Where is Jordan getting this pseudo-information?"

"I don't know," Brynn said. "I haven't told Jordan anything. He knows about the prank, but that was no secret. I've never mentioned the amethyst to him, or Alyssa's predictions, or anything like that."

Natalie uncrumpled the paper and reread Bunk Roundup. "Maybe he doesn't really know anything. If you read this carefully, it's all hints and guessing, but it doesn't say anything specific. And broomsticks? Please. That's way off the mark."

"Still, why would he write these hints in the first place?" Chelsea said. "Somebody must be talking to him. But what do they know? And if it's not Brynn, who is it?"

Everyone looked from Brynn to Alyssa to Natalie and back to Chelsea. Brynn read the same answer on all their faces. "Could it be?"

"Gaby?" Natalie said.

"I wouldn't put it past her," Alyssa said.

"But I thought she was reformed," Brynn said.

Chelsea shrugged. "Reformed? Maybe that was an act. Or just temporary. You can't ask a cat to stop being a cat. And you can't ask Gaby to turn saintly in a few short months."

"Actually, it's been eleven months," Brynn said. "Don't forget—you weren't so saintly yourself last summer."

"I'm an angel now," Chelsea said. "I swear!"

Brynn exchanged a look with Natalie and Alyssa. Chelsea did seem nicer this year, but she was in no position to rag on Gaby.

"If Gaby is leaking our secrets," Natalie said, "why is she doing it? What is she up to?"

"I don't know," Alyssa said. "But I do know she wants that amethyst—badly."

"Do you think we should confront her?" Natalie said.

"I do," Chelsea said. "Why not? Let's see how she reacts."

Shielding her eyes from the sun, Brynn peered out at the boats on the lake. "Gaby's boat is heading in now," she said.

Chelsea stood up. "No time like the present."

▲ ▲ ▲

Gaby found a small welcoming party—Alyssa, Natalie, Brynn, and Chelsea—waiting for her on the dock. Only they didn't look so welcoming. She was feeling low as it was, having accidentally dropped Donovan's boating shoe in the water while they were sailing that afternoon. (Luckily, the shoe floated. The leather would never be the same, but Donovan didn't seem too upset about it. At least he laughed.)

She had a bad feeling about this posse, but she decided to pretend everything was fine. "What's up, guys?"

"We need to talk to you," Chelsea said. Of course Chelsea had to be the enforcer.

"What about?" Gaby asked, but she was pretty sure she knew what about—the amethyst.

Donovan was tying up the Sunfish. Candace and Valerie were docking their boat. Gaby saw them look curiously at Gaby and her little welcoming party.

"Maybe we should go someplace private," Brynn said.

"Fine with me," Gaby said. They walked up the path to a small clearing in the woods. They sat on logs around a cold fire pit filled with ashes. Gaby shifted nervously on her log.

"What do you know about the pranking?" Chelsea asked.

"Nothing!" Gaby said. Why did they always blame her for everything? She was totally innocent! Well, pretty innocent.

"Alyssa says you were in the cabin when she got there—alone," Brynn said. "Why weren't you with the rest of us at the campfire?"

"I was cold," Gaby said. It was a lie, but it felt true. It was windy that night. She probably would have gotten cold. "I wanted to get my sweatshirt. So I ran back to the cabin, and when I walked in—*pow!* Everything was a wreck! Two seconds later Alyssa walked in, and then the rest of you." She couldn't tell them the whole truth—that she had planned to take Amy herself. What difference did it make now? She *didn't* prank the bunk, and she *didn't* take Amy. That was the important thing.

Alyssa shook her head. "Oh, Gaby. We thought you'd grown out of all your conniving and scheming. We thought you were reformed."

"But I am reformed!" Gaby cried. "I'm innocent! I didn't do it!"

The other girls just looked at one another sadly.

"Why don't you believe me?" Gaby said. "I'm telling the truth."

"Okay, Gaby," Natalie said. "Calm down."

"How can I? You all think I pranked my own bunk and stole Amy. But I didn't do it. And I'll prove it!"

"We better get going," Brynn said. "We've got that swim relay against 5C, and I have to change into my suit."

"We've got to beat them," Alyssa said. "To prove our obstacle course victory wasn't a fluke."

"And to avoid wearing swimsuits to the dance," Natalie reminded her.

"Are you going to bring your new super-athletic ability?" Chelsea asked Alyssa. "Or is it going to be the same old dorky Alyssa out there, thrashing around in the water, asking which way to the finish line?"

"Don't worry, I'll bring it," Alyssa said, but she looked kind of doubtful.

Gaby was grateful that they'd changed the subject. Better they pick on Alyssa than on her.

chapter
TEN

The Lakeview Tattler

Sports Update by Brynn

6B vs. 5C: The Rematch

After their humiliating defeat on the obstacle course two weeks ago, bunk 5C challenged 6B to a swim relay, which took place this afternoon. Let's just say the score is even now. As a member of 6B, I'd like to leave it at that, but it's my duty as a journalist to report the whole story, no matter how painful.

The two teams were neck and neck until the second-to-last lap, when 6B's Alyssa forgot to touch the wall after her swim. Thinking everything was okay, 6B's next swimmer, Candace, dove into the water to finish the race. She swam fast and edged 5C's last swimmer, Winnie, by a nose. 6B thought they'd won the relay, but they were wrong. The referee disqualified 6B because Alyssa never touched the wall at the end of her lap. 5C won on a heartbreaking technicality.

That means that we 6B-ers have to wear bathing suits to the Midsummer Dance! As many of you know, traditionally the sixth-division girls go formal to the dance, and a bathing suit is about as informal as you can get. But we have agreed to wear our suits under our dresses and dance in bathing suits to ONE SONG ONLY. The girls of 5C accepted this compromise after their counselor made them. Even they could see that depriving us of our one chance to wear the formal dresses we brought just for this occasion was too cruel.

Brynn paused at the keyboard and sighed. She'd stopped by the newspaper office after dinner that night to write up a report about the depressing swim relay that afternoon. 5C had cheered and high-fived after the meet. Winnie was nice enough to come over to the sixth-division girls and say, "Tough relay." It was a sportsmanlike gesture, Brynn guessed, but was there a hint of a sneer behind it? Was Winnie rubbing the victory in their faces?

Brynn got her answer when another 5C girl said, "See you at the dance, girls—in your Speedos."

Brynn bristled at the memory. Then she thought she heard a noise outside the office. Was someone out there? She froze, listening, but all she heard was a gang of boys trooping by on their way to the lodge.

She felt nervous at the newspaper these days. Weird things were going on. Like Jordan and Winnie's secret story. When was that going to come out? When would they at least tell the newspaper staff what they were working on?

Brynn had a bad feeling that secret story had something to do with bunk 6B.

And what about the blind item in Bunk Roundup? Who was the source of all the rumors?

She heard a noise again and swiveled around in her chair. Gaby stood in the doorway, silhouetted by the light on the path outside.

"I need your help," Gaby said.

"My help?" Brynn said. What could she do to help anyone? "What's up?"

"I'm innocent," Gaby said. "I didn't prank the bunk, and I didn't take Amy. But no one believes me."

Brynn didn't know what to say. Gaby did have a history of selfish behavior, even if she'd been better lately.

"You believe me, don't you, Brynn?" Gaby stood in front of Brynn, pleading, her eyes welling with tears. Or was that a trick of the light?

Brynn sighed. The thing was, she *did* believe Gaby. She wasn't sure why . . . something just told her Gaby didn't do it. Usually, when she was up to no good, Gaby radiated a sense of pride in her badness. Now she just seemed sad that no one trusted her.

"Yes," Brynn said. "I believe you."

"Then you have to help me prove my innocence," Gaby said. "You're a reporter. You know how to find things out, right?"

"Well . . ." Brynn really thought of herself as an actress. The newspaper was just one of her electives—though she had to admit, she was enjoying it.

"Help me find out who really took the amethyst," Gaby said. "We all want it back. It brought us good luck. I think we lost the swim meet today because we didn't have Amy."

"Really?"

"Remember how great Alyssa was in the obstacle course?" Gaby said. "That was right after she found Amy. She started having fantastic luck. Now Amy's gone, and Alyssa forgets to touch the wall in a race? How weird is that?"

"It's not that strange," Brynn said. "Alyssa's not exactly a jock."

"She was when she had Amy," Gaby said.

Hmm. Brynn had wondered herself whether

Amy brought good luck. Then there was Winnie and the weird secrets at the paper. Were they connected to the prank? To the amethyst? Maybe Brynn should look into it. After all, she was a reporter now.

"All right," she said. "I'll help you. Something strange is going on, and I want to find out who's behind it and why."

"Excellent," Gaby said. "You start interviewing suspects. I'll snoop around a little."

"Don't do anything too, you know, unethical," Brynn said.

"Hey," Gaby said. "We're a team. The unethical part is what you need me for."

Brynn flinched, but Gaby was right. Sometimes you had to fight sneakiness with sneakiness. And Gaby was the queen of sneaky.

▲ ▲ ▲

"Anybody want to listen to the Phillies game on the radio tonight?" Jenna asked at lunch the next day. Natalie was only half listening to the conversation. She was distracted by Logan, who sat across the mess hall with the boys in his bunk. He was totally staring at her. She stared back, and he looked away.

"I want to hear the game," Alex said, but most of the other girls shrugged, including Natalie. She wasn't a huge baseball fan.

"What's the point of getting all worked up about the Phillies if we can't go to the game next week?" Natalie said.

"That's true." Jenna looked dejected.

"You can always change your minds and go,"

Mandy said. "There's still time."

"No way," Chelsea said. "I'm not a big believer in Alyssa's psychic powers, but my face is too beautiful to be creamed by a baseball. I'm not taking chances."

"What's your prediction on the game tonight, Alyssa?" Sloan asked. "Will the Phillies beat Arizona?"

"Baseball's not exactly my specialty," Alyssa said.

"Oh, come on, just a guess," Priya said. "You can do it."

"Well, okay," Alyssa said. "The Phillies will win. But don't make any bets based on that."

"It's just fun to see if you'll be right or not," Brynn said.

Natalie looked up from her turkey sandwich. Logan was staring at her again. At first she thought it was a coincidence that he just happened to be looking in her direction. But after a few more bites and a sip of apple juice, she checked again, and he was still staring. What a weirdo.

"What is his problem?" She nudged Alyssa, who turned around. "He is staring at me, right? I'm not imagining it?"

"You're not imagining it," Alyssa said. "He's staring."

Logan looked away. Whew. Natalie wasn't sure why his staring made her feel uncomfortable. Maybe it was because she couldn't figure out what it meant. He ran away from her every time she came near him. And he wasn't shy, she knew that for certain. So why stare at her now? Did he hate her or something? Was he casting some kind of spell on her?

No, probably not casting a spell, she thought. That was Alyssa's amethyst talk getting to her. Still, it was annoying.

When she'd finished her lunch, she got up to bus her tray. Logan's campers were busy cleaning up their table. Logan was looking at Nat.

Well, that's it, she thought. She tossed her trash in the garbage and marched over to him.

"What do you think you're doing?" she demanded.

He went pale, which wasn't easy considering how tan he was. "Nothing," he said. "Eating lunch."

"Why are you staring at me?" she said.

"Staring?"

"Yes," Natalie said. "You've been staring at me all through lunch."

"N-no reason," Logan said, stammering slightly. Stammering was totally out of character for him. Logan was confident, a cool guy. He didn't stammer.

"There must be something going on," Natalie said. "Are you mad at me?"

"Not at all."

"Is there something weird on my face? Ketchup on my chin? The mark of Satan on my forehead? A 'kick me' sign on my back?"

"No, Nat. Really. I wasn't staring. I'm too busy to stare. See?" He grabbed one of his little charges and practically attacked the kid's face with a napkin. "Let's get you cleaned up, all right, buddy?" he said.

The boy squirmed. "But you already wiped my face off five minutes ago."

"Well, it got dirty again." He glanced up at Nat. "See? Not staring. Nothing going on. Your bunk is leaving. You'd better get going."

She frowned at him for a few long seconds, but he refused to look up at her again. So she marched off, totally unsatisfied. He said he wasn't staring? A bald-faced lie! What was wrong with these stupid boys? Why did they all have to act like aliens?

▲ ▲ ▲

"Nice work today, Candace," Hank said after sailing that afternoon. "You too, Valerie. Donovan, you've got your work cut out for you."

Candace grinned. She'd been a good sailor most of her life, but sailing every day at camp was making her *really* good. And Valerie had turned out to be a great first mate—she caught on to everything very quickly.

"Gaby and I are faking you out," Donovan said. "We're just pretending to screw up, to give you a false sense of security. Right, Gabs?"

"Right. Totally." Gaby turned red. Poor Gaby. She was slowing Donovan down, and she must have been afraid he resented her for it. But Gaby had improved a lot. Candace thought Gaby was doing great, considering that when she started she didn't know the bow from the stern.

That day Donovan had called for another informal race around the buoys, and Candace and Valerie had blown past them from the start. Donovan and Gaby never had a chance to catch up. And from what Candace could see, Gaby hadn't done anything wrong. She was beginning to know her way around a Sunfish. But Candace had the faster boat that day, that was all there was to it.

"We are going to stun you at the regatta," Donovan said. He was joking around, but Candace had a feeling that deep down he was very competitive.

"Nice job from all of you," Hank said. "See you all tomorrow."

Candace tossed her life jacket in the storage bin and started back to the bunk with Valerie.

"Movie night tonight," Valerie said. "Are you going to vote for *Mean Girls* or *Cars*?"

Dr. Steve let the campers vote for the movie they wanted to see on movie night. Right before dinner he counted the ballots and announced the winner.

"*Mean Girls* or *Cars*?" Candace said. "*Mean Girls*, of course."

"I heard some fifth-division boys are rigging the election," Valerie said. "They're bribing the little girls to vote for *Cars*."

"Bribing them? With what?" Candace asked.

"Popsicles," Valerie said.

"Popsicles. We can do better than that," Candace said. "Doesn't somebody have a box of Mallomars around somewhere?"

"Jenna does," Valerie said. "She's organizing a posse to stop the little girls on their way to the ballot box and show them the error of their ways. Want to come?"

"Sure I want to come," Candace said. "I'll meet you up there."

They parted at a fork in the path. Candace

walked on toward her bunk, past a pretty clearing with a small gazebo and a few benches surrounded by honeysuckle.

"Hey, Candace!" Donovan chased after her up the path. "Wait up a second."

She stopped. What could Donovan want with her? She must have left her stopwatch on the dock or something . . .

"Nice sailing today," he said. His hands were empty. No stopwatch.

"Thanks," Candace said. "You too."

"I've got some work to do if I'm going to beat you," he said. "But I *will* beat you."

"You'll beat us? We'll see," Candace said. She waited for him to say something else. It was awkward. They stepped out of the way so two counselors could jog past them.

"Can I ask you something?" Donovan said.

"Ask me something? Sure," Candace said.

He gestured toward the benches. "Want to sit down a minute?"

"Okay." What on earth was this about? Donovan had hardly said two words to her since the first day of camp. Okay, he'd said a few more words than that, but they were always along the lines of, "Let's race," or "My boat's going to whip your boat's butt." He spent most of his time fending off other girls.

Candace sat on a bench. The smell of pine and honeysuckle filled the clearing.

"Um, sorry," he said. "I'm a little nervous."

"Nervous?" she said. "About what?"

"About, like, asking people stuff," Donovan

said, suddenly uncharacteristically shy.

"You don't have to be nervous around me," Candace said.

"Thanks," he said. "I mean, I know that. That's why I like you."

Even after he said those words, "I like you," Candace didn't get it. The full meaning didn't sink in until later, after she'd turned that moment over again and again in her mind. At the time she just thought he meant, "I respect your sailing ability."

She didn't say anything. She sat still, waiting to hear what he wanted. Tacking tips? Hints on rigging? She wasn't about to give away any of her secrets, that was for sure.

"I was wondering . . . if you'd go to the Midsummer Dance with me."

Candace blinked. The what now? Did he say something about the regatta?

No, he didn't. He'd asked her to the dance.

Candace felt a slight shock. *Just as Alyssa had predicted!*

Wow. This was major. This was fate! She had vowed to stay boy-free all summer, to concentrate on sailing. But Alyssa had said Donovan would ask her to the dance. And now, because of sailing, he had! Life sure was weird.

"I caught you off guard, didn't I?" Donovan said. "Sorry about that. I just . . . I've met a lot of girls since I got to camp, and I know this dance is a big deal and all, and I thought you'd be the most fun girl to hang out with. At the dance. So what do you say? You're being kind of quiet."

"Quiet. Sorry!" Candace was flustered and confused. What should she say? Her head was spinning.

"See, it's just that . . ." Donovan shifted on the bench and played with his fingers. "Ever since I got to camp, a lot of girls have been kind of . . . hanging around me."

Candace laughed. "Hanging around? You mean chasing you."

Donovan laughed, too. "Okay, chasing me. And they're all really nice, but, well, I don't like being chased. It gets tired."

"I guess it could get old," Candace said. "Not that I know from personal experience or anything . . ." She had never been the type of girl boys went crazy over.

"You haven't chased me at all," Donovan said. "And you're such a great sailor, we have so much in common . . . I just think you're the coolest girl here. So . . . will you go with me?"

Wow, she thought again. Donovan seemed like such a great guy. But what about her promise to her parents?

She decided to be honest with him. That usually kept her out of trouble. "Um, can I think this over for a little while?" she said. "I like you and everything, it's not that. But my parents are putting a lot of pressure on me to focus on college-related stuff, and they don't want me dating any boys. Too distracting. So I kind of promised them . . ."

"But they're not here, right?" Donovan said. "It's just a dance."

"I know, but—"

He stood up. "It's okay. Think about it. I under-stand."

"Thanks, Donovan. I appreciate that."

He trotted off, as if in a hurry to get somewhere. Candace walked slowly back to the bunk. She forgot all about helping Jenna and Valerie rig the movie vote. She hoped she'd find somebody in the cabin, and she was in luck. Alyssa, Natalie, Tori, Chelsea, Mandy, and Gaby were all there, reading, trying on makeup, and playing cards.

Alyssa looked up from her book when Candace walked in. Candace knew she must have had an odd expression on her face, because Alyssa immediately said, "Candace, what happened?"

Candace flopped down onto her bunk, feeling happy and confused. "Donovan asked me to the dance."

Everyone gasped. Then, for a moment, total silence reigned in bunk 6B. But only for a moment.

"Oh my gosh!"

"Alyssa was right again! I don't believe it!"

"Is it true?" Gaby stood over Candace's bunk, staring down at her. "Tell me you're kidding around."

Candace felt a pang of guilt. She'd forgotten about Gaby's monster crush on Donovan. Of course this news would upset her.

"I'm sorry, Gaby," she said. "It's true."

Alyssa jumped onto Candace's bunk. The other girls gathered around. "What did you say?" Alyssa asked.

"She said yes, of course," Natalie said. "This is Donovan we're talking about."

"Actually, I told him I'd think about it," Candace said.

"Are you crazy?" Alyssa said. "Why?"

"Well, what about my vow?" Candace said. "I promised myself no boys this summer. That means no dates to the dance, doesn't it?"

"Good thinking," Mandy said. "You have a good head on your shoulders, Candace. Boys can be distracting."

Tori rolled her eyes. "Vows are made to be broken. Especially when the cutest boy at camp asks you out!"

"Hey," Gaby said. "Don't talk her out of her vow. If she wants to be a nun all summer, that's her business. And that puts Donovan right back on the market."

"I agree," Chelsea said. "Candace was never that interested in Donovan in the first place, right? So why should she pretend to like him when she doesn't even want a boyfriend?"

"It's not that I don't like him," Candace said. "He's a great sailor. And he's really nice. I guess I just wasn't thinking about him that way. In a crush way, I mean."

"But now you are, right?" Alyssa said. "I mean, now that you know he likes you, doesn't that make you think of him differently?"

"I guess," Candace said. "I need a little time to get used to the idea."

"So what are you going to do?" Gaby asked.

"I don't know," Candace said. "What do you all think I should do?"

"Go to the dance with him," Tori said.

"Definitely," Natalie said.

"I'll support you no matter what you decide," Mandy said. "But I think your vow is a smart idea."

"Listen to our fearless leader," Chelsea said. "Don't go."

"Gaby?" Candace asked.

"You really want my opinion?" Gaby said. "Because I'll say right up front I'm totally biased."

"Give it to me anyway."

"Okay," Gaby said. "Don't go. If you're not crazy wild for him like half the girls at camp, maybe you shouldn't be the chosen one."

"Maybe that's why he likes her," Tori said. "Because she's the only girl who's not throwing herself at him. The only one without a boyfriend, anyway."

Gaby frowned.

"What about you, Alyssa?" Candace asked. In her mind, Alyssa's opinion carried the most weight. Since she'd found Amy, Alyssa had made so many amazing predictions. Including this one, which Candace would never have foreseen in a million years. Alyssa seemed to have a halo of wisdom over her head.

"It's totally your decision," Alyssa said.

Candace pressed her. "But what's your advice?"

"Well, when I had the amethyst, I saw you with Donovan," Alyssa said. "That makes me think you should be with him. The way I think of it, your vow is fine for ordinary boys, but Donovan is no ordinary boy. For all we know, he may be the love of your life."

"That's so romantic," Natalie said.

"So my advice is, for Donovan, forsake the vow," Alyssa said. "Amy has spoken. Or would speak, if she were here. She was right about this, wasn't she? And everyone doubted us."

"Go to the dance with him," Tori said. "It won't kill you."

Nat and Tori clapped with excitement. Gaby looked downcast.

"I still think you should stick to your first decision, Candace," Mandy said. "On the other hand, it's always fun to have a date to a dance." She went back to her cot and opened the book she was reading.

"I'm with Mandy," Chelsea said. "Everybody is way too impressed with Alyssa's amethyst. Candace, you made a promise to yourself. Are you really going to break that promise because Alyssa says a rock told you to?"

"Yeah," Gaby said. "Are you going to let a rock rule your life?"

"But she's always right." Candace felt confused. "I need to think this over."

Candace hadn't believed in the amethyst's powers at first, but so much had happened since then, and Alyssa and Amy had predicted all of it. Their success ratio was one hundred percent. It seemed foolish to bet against them. What if Alyssa was right and Donovan was the love of her life? How could she walk away from the love of her life?

"Hey," Gaby said. "Who won that baseball game last night, anyway? The one between the Phillies and somebody?"

"The Arizona Cardinals," Mandy called from

her cot across the room. "The Cardinals won."

Candace looked at Alyssa. Everyone did. Alyssa went pale and picked at a thread on Candace's pillowcase.

"Hey," Chelsea said. "You picked the Phillies to win."

"That's right," Gaby said. "You did."

"You were wrong," Chelsea said. "Miss Psychic Hotline finally got one wrong."

"I—I know," Alyssa said. "Nobody's perfect, right?"

"So you might not be psychic?" Gaby said. "You might just be a regular schmo like us?"

Alyssa flashed Gaby a suspicious look, and Candace caught it. What was that about?

"I *am* psychic," Alyssa said. "I sometimes get a strong feeling about what's going to happen in the future. But no one bats a thousand."

"Speaking of bats, what about the field trip?" Chelsea said. "To the Phillies game? You saw a pretty clear vision of me getting smacked. Are you saying you might be wrong?"

"Anything's possible," Alyssa said. "But that dream felt very clear to me."

"Also, you had the amethyst stashed under your pillow that night," Gaby said. "Maybe it heightens your psychic powers."

Alyssa shot Gaby another odd look. Was that because she suspected Gaby of taking the amethyst?

"I'm just saying," Gaby said.

"Just saying . . . I wonder who took Amy," Candace said. "Do you think we'll ever get her back?"

"I hope so," Alyssa said.

"The baseball game is only a few days away," Mandy said. "We can still go if we want to. There's nothing stopping us."

"Do you all want to change your minds?" Alyssa asked.

"No," Natalie said.

"No," Tori said.

"No," Candace said. "Your prediction about Donovan has me spooked. It's too eerie."

"I agree," Chelsea said. "I can't go to the game now. It feels too dangerous."

"Alyssa has been right too many times," Gaby said.

"Okay, suit yourselves." Mandy blew a strand of hair off her face. "Next year I'm going to request a less superstitious group of girls."

chapter

ELEVEN

"So, what have you heard about our bunk?" Brynn was interviewing Jordan as part of her ongoing investigation into the missing amethyst. She'd found him outside the main lodge and sat him down on the steps for a little talk. "Tell me everything you know. Who's your source for that ridiculous gossip in Bunk Roundup?"

"Brynn, you're a reporter," Jordan said. "You know I can't reveal my sources."

Brynn took a deep breath. This was important. She needed to muster all her strength. *I'm a reporter,* she told herself. *I can do this. I can get the information I need, even out of a seasoned camp newsman like Jordan.*

Besides being a reporter, Brynn was an actress. And that was a skill that could also come in handy right about now . . .

"You're right, Jordan," she said. "I'm a reporter. And you're a reporter. We're both dedicated to finding the truth. Right?"

"Right."

"I understand about protecting your sources," Brynn said in her most coaxing yet serious "we're all professionals here" voice. "But I'm not the enemy. I'm your colleague. We both work on the same paper. We should help each other out, not compete against each other, or keep secrets from each other."

Jordan tapped his feet on the bottom step. He was breaking down, she could feel it. If there was one thing Brynn knew, it was her Jordan.

"Tell you what," Brynn said. She remembered a scene from an old movie she once saw, *All the President's Men*. It was about two reporters who did whatever they had to, including risking their lives, to bring down the President of the United States over some scandal. Maybe the amethyst situation wasn't as big, but someone had taken it, and as a result, Gaby had been falsely accused. Brynn was determined to find the stone and restore Gaby's honor. Besides, she'd been counting on Amy's good luck to help her get a starring role in the camp musical.

"I'll tell you who I think your secret source is," she said to Jordan. "And if I'm right, you tap your right foot. If I'm wrong, tap your left foot. Okay?"

"My source would kill me if she—or he—knew I revealed his or her identity," Jordan said carefully.

"You're not revealing anyone's identity," Brynn said. "All you're doing is tapping your foot. Perfectly innocent. I know you want to do the right thing, Jordan. And this is the right thing for everyone. Did you ever see *All the President's Men?*"

Jordan nodded. "Those reporters are my heroes."

"Me too," Brynn said. It was a lie, though. Her real heroes were Amanda Bynes and Keira Knightly.

But she did admire the *All the President's Men* guys as well. "They were willing to make any sacrifice for the greater good."

"I should be more like them, shouldn't I?" Jordan asked.

"Yes," Brynn said. "You definitely should."

He didn't say anything, just tapped his feet again, which she took as his signal that he was ready for questioning.

"Okay," Brynn said. "Who told you about the strange goings-on in our bunk? Was it . . . Logan?" She knew it couldn't be Logan. She just threw that in there to make it look like she didn't already have a very strong suspicion of who the culprit was. To throw Jordan off guard.

Jordan tapped his left foot.

"Was it Chelsea?" She didn't believe it was Chelsea, either. But Jordan might believe she believed it. Chelsea was a plausible suspect, since she was anti-Amy.

Jordan tapped his left foot.

Now for the moment of truth. "Was it Winnie?"

Jordan's right toes lifted. He hesitated. Then he tapped his right foot, once.

Aha! So it was Winnie. Brynn had had a bad feeling about that girl from the beginning.

"I knew it," Brynn said. "But no one in 6B is friends with Winnie. What does she know? And how did she find out?"

"She overheard some girls from your bunk talking," Jordan said. His reluctance to give away his secrets seemed to have disappeared. He looked almost relieved to talk. "At the cookout that first day. All she heard was something about an amazing magic phenomenon, something having to do with Alyssa. But that's all Winnie picked up. She told me about it and convinced me we should investigate."

"What else did you find out in your investigation?" Brynn asked.

"Not much," Jordan said. "You sixth-division girls sure stick together. Nobody would talk. Not even Gaby. And she's got a pretty big mouth."

Brynn felt proud of her bunkmates. They'd all stuck to their supersworn vows of silence—in spite of their differences.

"What about the pranking?" she said. "Was that you? Were you looking for clues or something?"

Jordan shook his head. "I'd never do that. I don't know who pranked your bunk."

"Could Winnie have done it on her own?" Brynn asked. "Maybe she ransacked the cabin while looking for clues, and then made it look like a prank?"

"I don't know," Jordan said. "I wouldn't put it past her. She'd do anything for a story. She got pretty fed up with me because I didn't want to spy on Alyssa."

Spy on Alyssa! That Winnie was even worse than Brynn had thought. But what about the amethyst? Did Jordan know about it?

"If Winnie found a clue, or something like that, in our bunk, do you think she would take it?"

Jordan shrugged. "Maybe. She hasn't mentioned finding anything or taking anything."

"So that's all you know?" Brynn said.

"That's all I know. I still have no idea what you girls are up to. If Winnie knows more, she hasn't told me. I'm not sure she trusts me anymore. Or maybe she wants to grab all the glory for herself when she finally breaks the story."

"You mean, *if* she breaks the story," Brynn said.

"I mean *when*," Jordan said. "That girl's like a bulldog—she goes after what she wants."

"I'll remember that," Brynn said. So Jordan didn't know about Amy. That meant he didn't know what had happened to her, either. But Brynn had a feeling maybe Winnie did.

"Good work, Brynn," Gaby said. Brynn had come to her with an update on the missing amethyst mystery. They met for a secret rendezvous in the arts and crafts room just before dinner. If anyone caught them, they could just say they had a sudden, irresistible urge to make boxes out of Popsicle sticks.

"I don't have proof of anything," Brynn said. "Just a few suspicions. And I'm pretty sure Jordan had nothing to do with it."

"But Winnie did," Gaby said. "I'm sure of it."

"She might have," Brynn said. "But she'll never admit it. How will we prove it?"

"Easy," Gaby said. "We just break into Winnie's bunk and look around." Why didn't other people see the obvious solutions that were so clear to her? Was it because they had scruples?

"Break into 5C?" Brynn said. "We can't do that. It's against the rules."

"So?" Gaby said. "Breaking into *our* bunk was against the rules, too, but somebody did that."

"I can't," Brynn said. "My journalistic principles don't allow for breaking and entering."

"Ugh," Gaby said. "Journalistic principles? Where did you get that? What is journalism about? *Finding out stuff.* What's the best way to find out stuff? *Snoop through people's things.* Basic logic."

"Well, there's also asking people questions," Brynn said.

"But you already admitted that won't work in this case. Look, you don't want to do it, fine. *I* don't have any journalistic principles, so I will."

"When?"

"Tonight. The fourth division is putting on some kind of skit in the theater. The whole camp will be there. It's the perfect time for crime."

"Okay," Brynn said. "I don't like this. But I'm secretly glad you're doing it. Taking one for the team."

"You got it."

"Be careful."

"I so totally will."

⛺ ⛺ ⛺

The fourth division's skit about oral hygiene, starring Declan the Decayer, was a total snoozefest, so Gaby didn't mind at all sneaking out of the theater in the middle of it. "Bathroom break," she whispered to Mandy, who looked up when she started for the door. And that was it. Easy as pie. She was out of there.

The camp was quiet, the cabins dark. Gaby

found her way to 5C and pushed open the door. *Creak*. She hadn't expected snooping to be so spooky.

She clicked on her flashlight and got to work. Right away she homed in on a cubby marked WINNIE and rifled through it. Nothing interesting there, beyond a suspicious amount of chocolate. Did Winnie have a little chocoholic problem? That was good information in case Gaby ever needed blackmail material later.

Gaby shined the flashlight around the room. If Winnie didn't keep important secret amethysts in her cubby—which made sense, it was too obvious and the first place someone would look (Gaby kicked herself for falling into the trap)—where would she hide them? Under her mattress, perhaps? But which bed was Winnie's?

Gaby patted beds and felt under pillows until she found something lumpy. She reached under a mattress, but it was only someone's photo album. Gaby flipped through it. It showed another 5C girl, Gwenda, with her family and friends from home. Not what Gaby was looking for. She put the album back where she found it and kept searching.

At last she caught sight of something odd, high up on the wall near a top bunk. She climbed up to investigate. A piece of paper stuck out from behind a loose board. Gaby pulled the board back. Aha! A hiding place! With two books stuffed inside.

Gaby took out the books. She felt around the space to make sure there was no amethyst there, but came up empty.

She opened the first book. It was a reporter's

notebook, with PROPERTY OF WINNIE JACKSON written on the front. Jackpot!

Gaby opened it and flipped through a few boring pages of notes about reporting techniques before she got to the good stuff.

bunk 6B—Alyssa. Psychic? How?

6B girls keep to themselves a lot. Always whispering, having secrets. What are they up to?

Bunk 6B crossed names off sign-up sheet for Phillies game. Why? Up to something? Do they know something we don't? Will we come back from game to face some kind of evil superprank?

Brynn—went out with Jordan last year? Yes. Interesting. She seems drippy. What did he see in her? Does he still like her? Can't tell. She obviously likes him, tho.

Heard 6B girls talking about Alyssa again, and someone named Amy. Who is Amy???? Must find out.

Amy Goldberg—little girl in second div.—the Amy 6B girls obsessed with? Seems unlikely. Could Amy Goldberg be psychic?

Gaby laughed as she read. Winnie was obsessed with bunk 6B. And totally on the wrong track. Amy Goldberg—psychic? That little girl with the lisp? What are the odds?!

Next she looked at the second book. *The Smart Girl's Guide to Astrology.* Hmm. Gaby opened it up. On the first page, Alyssa had written her name. The book belonged to Alyssa!

Where would Winnie have gotten Alyssa's astrology book? Gaby was sure Alyssa wouldn't have given it to Winnie. Alyssa didn't even know her.

Winnie must have taken it from our bunk, Gaby

thought. This was proof that Winnie was up to something. But what about the amethyst? Did Winnie have that, too? Gaby looked around some more. She checked the cubbies again. She did find a few rocks, which was strange. They were in a box in the cubby marked GWENDA. Gaby looked them over carefully. None of them were Amy. She knew for sure because each rock was marked with its type: mica, smoky quartz, jade, marcasite, malachite, agate . . . The spot marked AMETHYST was empty.

So Gaby didn't find Amy. That didn't mean Winnie hadn't hidden the amethyst somewhere. It didn't matter. Gaby had enough evidence to bust Winnie now—and to prove her own innocence. All those girls who didn't believe her would feel awfully sorry.

chapter
TWELVE

"Alyssa . . . Alyssa . . ."

Alyssa sat up. Was someone calling her name?

"Alyssa . . . Alyssa . . ."

The bunk was dark. Everyone else was sleeping soundly. So who was calling to her?

"Alyssa . . . Alyssa . . . It's me, Amy! Your long lost Amy!"

Amy! At last. Alyssa had missed the amethyst so much. And her psychic powers even more. "Amy, where are you?"

"Here I am. Can't you see me?"

Alyssa looked around. There was a big bushy wig on the floor. What was that doing there? Who wore a wig at camp?

"Alyssa, under here!"

The wig shook slightly. Alyssa thought she glimpsed Amy underneath it. But Alyssa was way up high on her top bunk. She tried to climb down, but her legs were frozen. She reached toward the floor with her arms, but it was too far. She could hear Amy calling, but she couldn't reach her . . .

"Amy! Amy! I'll find you!"

Alyssa woke up with a start. The morning sun made a square pattern through the window on the floor. Amy! Where was she?

Alyssa looked around for a shaggy wig, but there wasn't one anywhere. The only thing she saw on the floor was a pair of sneakers.

Amy had called to her. But it was only a dream.

Still, Alyssa couldn't shake the feeling that Amy really was calling to her. That her dream meant something. Her unconscious mind, or Amy's psychic vibes, were trying to send her a clue.

Alyssa climbed out of bed. The others were just waking up. Alyssa slipped on her flip-flops and started for the door.

"Where are you going?" Mandy asked.

"I'm not sure," Alyssa said. "But don't worry, I won't go far."

She didn't know where she was going or what exactly she was looking for, but something told her to go outside.

"Stay within sight of the cabin," Mandy called.

"I will," Alyssa said.

She walked around the cabin to the wall where Amy's hiding place had been. Just for kicks, she checked the nook again. Empty.

She stepped back and looked at the bunk, the window, the shutters slightly ajar, the bushes around the cabin . . .

The bushes! A round, shaggy boxwood sat right under Alyssa's window. And it was exactly the same shape as the wig in her dream! A breeze shook the bush. Alyssa could practically hear it calling to her—*Here I am! Here I am!*

She crawled under the bush and pawed through the loose dirt . . . and there was Amy! Right under the hiding nook, safe and sound.

Alyssa snatched up the amethyst and held it tight. "I found her!" she cried, and ran inside the bunk. "Everybody—look! I found Amy!"

"That's great!" Natalie cried, her mouth full of toothpaste. The other girls gathered around to look. Amy was slightly dirty, but otherwise no worse for wear. Alyssa polished Amy with her T-shirt.

"Where did you find it?" Mandy asked.

"Under a bush outside," Alyssa said. "I had a dream this morning that she was calling to me, and when I woke up, somehow I knew exactly where to find her." She rubbed the stone until the purple parts shone. "She really does have some kind of magic."

"But how did she get outside?" Valerie asked.

"I hid her in a nook behind the shutter." Alyssa showed them the hiding place. She wouldn't be using it anymore, anyway. It was too shallow, clearly not safe. "When we had that storm last week, the wind must have knocked her out of her nook. It just happened to be the same night our cabin got pranked."

"How do you know the wind did it?" Chelsea said. "Gaby could have taken Amy and hidden her under the bush."

"I didn't, though," Gaby said. She and Brynn exchanged a look.

"I believe her," Alyssa said. "First of all, why

would Gaby hide Amy under a bush? It's a stupid hiding place."

"That's right," Gaby began. "I—"

"Maybe Gaby knew you'd think that," Chelsea said. "She must have known that if you found Amy under the bush, you'd *think* the wind knocked her down—and you wouldn't blame Gaby."

Alyssa shook her head. Chelsea was being extra annoying this morning. "I just know she didn't." She squeezed Amy tight. "Amy is telling me."

Gaby said, "If I could just—"

Chelsea rolled her eyes. "Puh-lease."

"What about the pranking, though?" Valerie said. "The rainstorm didn't do that—and we still don't know who's responsible."

"Would you guys please let me talk?" Gaby said. "I have some very interesting information about the prank."

"What?" Alex said.

"Maybe we do know who did it," Gaby said. She reached under her bunk and pulled out Alyssa's astrology book.

"Hey—that's mine!" Alyssa said. "Where did you get it?"

"I found it in bunk 5C," Gaby said.

"What were you doing in bunk 5C?" Mandy asked.

"Nothing worse than what *they* did to *us*," Gaby said. "One of them, anyway. Specifically, Miss Winnie Jackson."

Everyone gasped. "How do you know for sure?" Brynn said.

"I found this book hidden near her bed," Gaby said. "She also has a notebook full of notes about our bunk. She overheard some of us talking about the amethyst and was trying to figure out what was going on—so she could write about it in the newspaper!"

"Gaby," Mandy said. "Did you sneak into bunk 5C without permission?"

"All I did was look around a little bit," Gaby said. "I did what I had to do. Look, Winnie messed up our cabin. She stole Alyssa's book. That's why she pranked us—she was looking for the amethyst and made it look like a prank to cover her tracks."

"Nice work, Gaby," Brynn said.

"I don't know," Chelsea said. "How do we know Gaby's telling the truth? Maybe *she* took Alyssa's book. Maybe *she* messed up the cabin looking for the amethyst. And now she's trying to blame it all on some innocent 5C girl."

"Innocent?" Alyssa said. "The same girls who threatened to kick our butts after we beat them on the obstacle course? Who are gloating over their swim relay victory? Gaby's story makes perfect sense to me."

"I believe her, too," Brynn said. "Winnie's been acting strange ever since we got to camp this summer. Even Jordan said she'd do anything for a story. And you know what? I think I'll go confront her right now." She grabbed the astrology book. "Can I borrow this?"

"Go ahead," Alyssa said. "Go, Brynn!" It felt so good to have the amethyst back and all her friends behind her.

"Don't do anything foolish!" Mandy called after her as Brynn marched out the door.

Chelsea laughed. "You might as well say 'Don't breathe.' This whole bunk has lost their minds."

"Chelsea, when are you going to admit there's something special about this amethyst?" Alyssa said.

"When I see real proof," Chelsea said.

"What kind of proof?" Alyssa asked.

"The impossible kind," Chelsea said. She snatched up the amethyst and tossed it in the air like a coin. But Alyssa snatched it back right before Chelsea caught it.

▲ ▲ ▲

Brynn knocked on the sky blue door of bunk 5C. Their counselor answered. "Is Winnie here?" Brynn asked.

"She went to the newspaper office," the counselor said. "To work on some story before breakfast."

"Thanks." Brynn hurried up the path to the newspaper office. She burst in and found Winnie and Jordan working together on one of the computers.

"Hey, Brynn," Jordan said.

"Hi, Jordan," Brynn said. "I need to talk to your partner about some of her unethical journalistic practices."

"What?" Jordan looked at Winnie, who blanched.

"I don't know what you're talking about," Winnie said.

"I think you do." Brynn held up *The Smart Girl's Guide to Astrology*. "One of our investigators found this in your bunk. Care to explain?"

"What? I've never seen that before in my life," Winnie said.

"Then what was it doing hidden next to your bed?" Brynn said. "With your reporter's notebook?"

"What? What were you doing snooping around my bed?"

"I personally didn't snoop," Brynn said. "But since you were the one who snooped first, it seems like fair payback."

Winnie lowered her eyes and twisted her fingers together. Then she glanced guiltily from Jordan to Brynn.

"All right," she said. "I admit it. I knew something big was going on in your bunk, but no matter how much asking around I did, no one would tell me what it was. I couldn't stand not knowing! I still don't know. It's driving me crazy!"

Brynn suppressed a grin. This confession was too sweet. But she didn't want to look like she was gloating over Winnie's defeat—especially in front of Jordan.

"So I snuck into your bunk to look around a little," Winnie said. "I emptied half your cubbies looking for clues. That's all I meant to do. I didn't want to steal anything or cause any damage. But then I accidentally knocked over a couple bottles of nail polish and I was afraid someone would notice. And I'd made such a mess and I couldn't remember where everything went . . . so I messed the place up even more, hung some underwear up, and made it look like a prank."

"And you wrote 'You've been pranked' on our bathroom mirror just in case we didn't get the message," Brynn said.

"Uh, yeah."

"Why did you steal Alyssa's book?"

"I didn't mean to steal it," Winnie said. "I just wanted to borrow it. It was the only thing I found in the cabin that seemed connected with the mystery. I thought there might be a clue in the book. But I looked through it and it's just a bunch of horoscopes."

Jordan gaped at Winnie, his jaw hanging open. "I can't believe what a criminal mastermind you are," he said.

"Is that a good thing?" Winnie said.

"Maybe to some people . . ." Jordan said.

"I'm really sorry, Brynn," Winnie said. "I never meant to cause so much trouble for you guys. Please apologize to everyone in your bunk for me."

"Why don't you do it yourself?" Brynn said. "A public apology in *The Lakeview Tattler* would be nice."

"In *The Tattler*?" Winnie gulped.

"I think you should," Jordan said.

"I'll write it up after breakfast," Winnie said. She got to her feet. "Now I think I'd better get to the mess hall." She ran out, red-faced.

"Wow," Jordan said. "That was amazing. If Winnie was as good at detective work as you are, we might have cracked the mystery of bunk 6B story. But we still don't know what's going on with you guys."

"And you won't," Brynn said. "Until we're ready to tell the world. We supersSwore not to tell anyone. And impossible as it sounds, we all actually stuck to our vows."

"Well, I'm very impressed," Jordan said. "You're one heck of a reporter, Brynn. Smarts and moxie all rolled up in one very cute girl."

"Thank you." Brynn blushed. Was Jordan flirting with her? His praise made her bold. "Speaking of detective work," she said. "I have a little question for you. Are you and Winnie just a reporting team, or is there something . . . I don't know . . ." Now the words were hard to say, but she forced herself. ". . . something *more* going on?"

"Something more?" Jordan said. "No. There never was. And now we're not even reporting partners. I don't want to work with someone who has such low standards. Though I'm pretty sure she learned her lesson."

"Let's hope so." Brynn regretted the pompous sound of her voice. Why be so high-handed about it? She knew Winnie wouldn't pull a stunt like that again.

chapter
THIRTEEN

Alyssa checked the little purse at her hip to make sure Amy was still there. She'd decided to carry the stone with her whenever possible. If she had to go swimming or something like that, she'd leave the amethyst in her pillowcase. Her bunkmates had proven that she could trust them.

Mandy herded the bunk to breakfast, even though Brynn wasn't back yet from her showdown with Winnie. Alyssa was dying to know what happened.

Finally, as the pancakes were being served, Brynn strolled into the mess hall looking triumphant.

"All right!" Sloan said. "Something good happened."

"She has avenged me and restored my good name," Gaby muttered.

"What?" Alyssa said.

"Nothing," Gaby said.

Brynn sat down at the table. "Well?" Valerie asked. "What happened?"

"Winnie confessed to everything," Brynn said.

The table cheered.

"She knew something strange was going on in our bunk, so she searched it for clues," Brynn said. "All she found was Alyssa's astrology book. But she broke something by accident—"

"My nail polish?" Tori said.

Brynn nodded. "So she made the whole thing look like a prank. She confessed to everything except taking the amethyst. She didn't say anything about it. I don't think she knows it exists."

Alyssa patted her little purse protectively. Yep, Amy was still there.

"See?" Gaby said. "I told you I had nothing to do with any of this."

"Funny," Chelsea said. "It looked so much like something you'd dream up. The whole scheme felt like a Gaby Production."

"I totally believe Gaby." Alyssa rubbed Amy and got a strong Gaby-is-innocent vibe. "In my dream I just knew somehow that Amy rolled away on her own. She was lost, not stolen. We all owe Gaby an apology."

Everyone stared, silent. Apologize to Gaby? Somehow it just went against the grain. It was counterintuitive. It didn't feel right.

Gaby frowned. "I'm disappointed in you all. How could my own bunkmates not trust me?"

Alex rolled her eyes—and she wasn't the only one. "There are lots of reasons why we might not trust you, Gaby. You've done some pretty sneaky things in the past."

"But I've reformed," Gaby said. "At least, I'm in the process of reforming."

"Good for you," Mandy said.

"We're all glad," Valerie said.

"Let's apologize and leave Gaby alone now," Mandy said. "Clearly she did nothing wrong."

"*This* time," Chelsea said.

"Chelsea . . ." Mandy's voice took a tone of warning. She was a pretty tough counselor. Maybe that was a good thing, Alyssa thought.

"We're sorry, Gaby," Priya said.

"We're sorry," the others echoed.

"Thank you," Gaby said with a smug grin.

"This is all very nice," Mandy said. "But you're forgetting one important thing. And this is something you girls just do not seem to want to remember."

"What?" Brynn asked.

"The 'lost' poster," Mandy said. "It's still up on the mess hall porch. Someone in 5C is missing her amethyst, and Alyssa should give it back right away."

"5C," Gaby said. "Winnie's bunk. That's a weird coincidence."

"Or *is* it a coincidence?" Alyssa said. She wasn't so sure.

"Alyssa—" Now Mandy used her warning voice on her. Alyssa decided Mandy was a little *too* tough.

"All right," Alyssa said. "I'll find the owner and give the amethyst back."

"Right away?" Mandy said.

"Right away," Alyssa said.

As they walked back to the cabin, Sloan, Brynn, and Gaby caught up with Alyssa. "You can't give Amy back now," Gaby said. "Think of all the weird things that have happened lately. They're all connected to 5C. Winnie's bunk. What if this is a trick? Amy could fall into the wrong hands!"

"I know you're right," Alyssa said. "But what can I do? I promised."

"Well, there's no time to give it back now," Sloan said. "We've got swimming lessons in five minutes. You can do it after lunch."

"Good idea." Alyssa stashed Amy in her pillow-case and put on her bathing suit. Whoever owned the amethyst—if she really *did* lose it—had waited all this time to get it back. She could wait a few more hours.

That afternoon, a new edition of *The Lakeview Tattler* came out. Alyssa flipped through it on her way to nature, stopping on page three.

A Public Apology

I, Winnie Jackson, wish to apologize for any distress I may have caused the residents of bunk 6B. I didn't mean to scare them or mess up their things, but I did, and I'm sorry. I'm also sorry if any innocent parties were blamed for my actions. In my zeal to investigate a story,

I crossed a line and went too far. And to the camp at large I'd like to say, pranking might seem like innocent fun, but it can mess with people's heads. Don't do it.

Apologetically yours,

Winnie Jackson

Alyssa appreciated the apology, but she hardly found it comforting. Winnie Jackson was in bunk 5C. What if she put up the "lost" poster as part of her "investigation?" What if it was a trap, a trick to get Alyssa to give Winnie a chance to try the amethyst's powers?

Her fears were totally possible. On top of that, deep down Alyssa didn't want to give up Amy. She hated to admit it, but it was true. She'd missed her so much when she was lost. Now they were reunited again, only to be separated once more. Alyssa hated the thought of giving up Amy. That's all there was to it.

Who can blame me? she thought. Anyone who'd felt the connection she had with that stone would understand.

chapter
FOURTEEN

"Okay, girls," Mandy said. "I'm going to ask you one last time: Have you changed your minds about the baseball game? Can we please be sensible and go?"

Why does Mandy keep harping on this? Alyssa wondered. Nothing had changed since she'd had her dream of Chelsea's terrible baseball attack. To Alyssa, that dream was as indisputable as fact. Why would they change their minds?

"What's the alternative?" Priya asked.

"We stay here and help clean out the boat-house," Mandy said. "Or, if you prefer, we can weed the vegetable garden."

"Ohhhh." Everyone in bunk 6B groaned. Most of them cast annoyed glances at Alyssa.

"Cleaning or weeding," Gaby said. "That's a great way to spend a beautiful day like today."

"I told you, you can still change your minds."

All eyes were on Alyssa. "I don't think we should go. Sorry, guys."

"Alyssa's right," Natalie said. "It's just too big a risk."

"Suit yourselves," Mandy said.

"We might have a boring day," Alyssa said to her bunkmates. "But just think—we'll be saving Chelsea's life!"

"We sure better be," Chelsea said. "I didn't come to summer camp to miss baseball games and weed the vegetable garden."

▲ ▲ ▲

"Good job, girls," Mandy said. "The garden looks great. Hit the showers."

"Phew," Alyssa wiped a strand of damp hair from her face. It was another scorching day and weeding was hard work.

"That was rough," Brynn said.

"Good exercise, though," Alyssa said. She was determined to make the best of this situation. "And think how great the vegetables will taste now."

"I'm not crazy about vegetables in the first place," Chelsea said. "But I do think I sweated off about five pounds."

They trudged back to their bunk, tired and cranky. As they passed the main lodge, the first bus pulled in, just back from the baseball game. The bus doors opened and kids poured off, cheering and babbling with excitement.

"Who won?" Valerie shouted to the arriving campers.

"Philly!" Jordan said. He and David, Jenna's boyfriend, ran over to give them the rundown. "10–8. It was a great game. Both teams were knocking home runs left and right. And hey—guess who sang the national anthem?"

"Who?" Brynn asked.

"You'll never guess," David said.

"Kanye West?" Chelsea said mockingly.

"Close," Jordan said.

Alyssa felt her forehead break out in a sweat. *Close! How is that possible? It was just a dumb baseball game.*

"50 Cent?" Alyssa asked. She needed to determine exactly how close *close* was.

Both David and Jordan shook their heads. "OK, now you're overshooting a little."

"Maroon Five?" Brynn tried.

"Better than that," David said. "Give up?"

"Yes!" Alyssa said. "Tell us!"

"Justin Timberlake!" David said. "It was amazing!"

"Justin Timberlake!" Brynn cried. "You're lying."

"No way," Chelsea said. "Not my Justin!"

"I swear," Jordan said. "Justin Timberlake sang the National Anthem. We saw him with our own eyes!"

"Wow," Brynn said. "Justin! I love him."

"So do I," Chelsea said. "And we missed it! I can't believe we missed it!"

Alyssa didn't like the sound of this at all. Something important was missing from Jordan's game summary.

"But what about the terrible accident?" she said.

"What terrible accident?" Jordan said.

"Didn't someone get hit in the head by a baseball?" Alyssa said, a nervous feeling creeping into her neck. "Didn't one of the players knock the ball into the stands and seriously injure a spectator?"

"Huh?" Jordan said. "I didn't see anything like that. Did you see anyone get beaned at the game?" he asked David.

David shook his head. "Nothing like that happened."

"It had to," Alyssa said. "Maybe you missed it. They called an ambulance and took the victim out of the stadium on a stretcher?"

"Where did you hear this?" David said. "On the radio?"

Alyssa didn't say that she'd heard it in her own head. Because that would mean revealing the secret of Amy. It also might mean sounding a little wacko. "Um—I thought I heard a news report," she said. The other girls looked at one another, unsure what to say.

David looked at Jordan. The boys shrugged. "If anything like that happened, we totally missed it. And I don't see how we could have. It was a perfect baseball day. You girls really should have gone. Why didn't you go, anyway?"

"Um, we had things to do," Alyssa said.

"Yeah," Jenna said. "We had to *weed out* a few things."

The boys looked confused. "Whatever," Jordan said. "See you at dinner."

The Lakeview Tattler

Bunk Roundup

by Jordan

Campwide News: Saturday's trip to Philadelphia for the Phillies-Mets game was definitely one of the highlights of the summer. The game was tight, with the score going back and forth until the ninth inning, but local favorites Philly won handily, 10–8. The day was hot and sunny with a nice breeze, the hot dogs and pretzels were ballpark-perfect, and a good time was had by all, from the youngest campers to the oldest counselors. Best of all was the surprise, unannounced appearance of pop superstar Justin Timberlake to sing the National Anthem. The girls were screaming their heads off! He even tossed a few Phillies bandannas into the crowd, and the third division's own Becca Johanson caught one! She's having it framed and hanging it on her bunk wall. Thanks for a fantastic and memorable day, Dr. Steve!

Bunk 6B: For some unknown reason, the girls of 6B refused to attend Saturday's baseball game. No one can get a straight answer out of them as to why they didn't want to go, but rumors abound that tensions are flaring. This bunk continues to be a source of rumor and mystery. Your intrepid reporter conducted interviews with several 6B-ers in search of answers.

Reporter: Why didn't your bunk go to the game today?

Valerie: Um, next question.

Brynn: No comment.

Priya: I plead the fifth.

Alex: Why don't you ask Alyssa?

Gaby: We were trying to do something nice for somebody in our bunk.

Reporter: How does missing a ball game help anyone?

Gaby: If you don't get it, I can't explain.

Jenna: Why don't you ask Alyssa?

Sloan: The planets were not well aligned, and if we had gone, a terrible tragedy could have happened. We couldn't live with the guilt.

Reporter: I don't understand.

Sloan (pulling out and unfolding a pocket astrological chart): See this placement of Pluto? It was in the same place when Brad left Jen for Angelina *and* when Britney Spears shaved all her hair off. You see how serious that can be. You don't mess with Pluto in Sag while Mercury is retrograde.

Reporter: I still don't understand.

Sloan: Ask Alyssa.

Candace: I never really understood why we couldn't go, but everyone seemed to agree.

Natalie: We can't talk about it, but we had our reasons.

Tori: Ask Alyssa.

Chelsea: My life was in danger, okay? That's what they told me. I'm beginning to wonder now if it was ever true.

Alyssa: I'm afraid we can't talk about it publicly. The girls of bunk 6B would like to ask everyone at Lakeview to please respect our privacy during this difficult time.

There you have it, folks. As far as I can figure out, the 6B-ers stumbled on a conspiracy to threaten Chelsea's life if they went to the game. Why, we don't know, but they're clearly cowed, shaken, and afraid to talk. More on this story as it develops.

"We missed the best day of camp ever for nothing!" Chelsea shouted. She crumpled the newspaper into a ball and heaved it at Alyssa. Everyone else in the bunk threw paper at her, too. A hail of paper missiles rained on her head. Ten pairs of eyes glared at her. Alyssa's bunkmates were mad.

"There was no terrible accident," Priya said. "How do you explain this?"

"You don't understand," Alyssa said. "We changed the cosmic balance by not going to the game. If we had gone, Chelsea would have been hit.

But since we didn't go, fate made a U-turn and the accident didn't happen."

"Besides," Sloan said. "How could Chelsea get hit with a baseball if she wasn't at the game?"

Alyssa was grateful to have at least one ally. The rest of her bunkmates had been giving her the cold shoulder since everyone else got back from the game.

"I guess you have a point," Natalie said.

"A stupid point," Chelsea said. "We were crazy to fall for any of this mumbo jumbo. How could I get hit by a baseball? It's just not *me*."

"I think Alyssa makes sense," Sloan said. "You can't deny she has had an amazing record for accurate predictions all month. I'm not going to go against her now. Who knows, maybe we *did* avert some terrible tragedy."

"Puh-lease," Jenna said.

"Oh, girls," Mandy said. "I'm sorry we missed the game—*believe* me. I'm not a huge Justin Timberlake fan—" Her eyes drifted toward the poster over Chelsea's bed "—but anything's better than weeding. Still, what's done is done. Can't we put all this silliness behind us now?"

"It's not silly," Natalie said. "What about Donovan asking Candace to the dance? That was incredible. Nobody would have predicted that—but Alyssa did."

"Yeah," Sloan said. "And what about all the smaller stuff, the pasta salad at the cookout, the canceled swim relay, the pancakes for breakfast—"

"Alyssa could have smelled the pancakes before

we left for the mess hall," Priya said. "You couldn't miss the smell on the path. Maybe she wasn't aware she was smelling it, but it could have tipped her off."

"And having pasta salad at the cookout isn't such a stretch," Mandy said.

"And Donovan asking Candace to the dance kind of makes sense," Jenna said. "They're both really into sailing."

"But he flirted with every girl in camp except Candace," Brynn said.

"I have to admit, even I was shocked that he asked me," Candace said.

"Any decision on that yet, Candace?" Gaby asked.

"No, not yet," Candace said.

"Don't push her, Gaby," Brynn said.

"What about Tumtum?" Natalie said. "Alyssa interpreted my dream right even though she didn't know Tumtum had a tumor—*and* she correctly predicted he'd be okay."

"She had a fifty-fifty chance of getting that right," Chelsea said.

"And she never actually said your dog had a tumor," Mandy reminded them. "She said you were worried about someone at home. That could apply to almost anyone at some point."

"But she got it right at the right time," Sloan said. "That's the key."

The argument went on, getting more heated by the moment. By the end about half the bunk—Sloan, Gaby, Natalie, Valerie, and Brynn—still believed in Alyssa and Amy. But the rest of them had soured on the whole psychic/amethyst thing.

"We're skipping over one very important question," Mandy said. "Alyssa—have you returned the amethyst to its rightful owner yet?"

Gulp. "Not yet," Alyssa admitted. "Everyone was away at the game yesterday, and then there's been so much excitement about it—"

"No more excuses," Mandy said. "The amethyst is not yours and you have to give it back."

"But—but—it's a crime to give Amy away." Alyssa held the amethyst in her palm. She felt so connected to it. "Who else would know how to use her? Who else has the intuitive power? No one."

"I have to agree with Alyssa," Sloan said. "She and Amy were meant to be together."

"Alyssa, I know it's hard, but it's the right thing and you have no choice," Mandy said. "Find out who the owner is and give the rock back."

"Okay," Alyssa said. She muffled her face in her pillow. She was going to miss Amy so much.

chapter

FIFTEEN

"I was thinking," Valerie said to Candace when they were out on the lake practicing sailing maneuvers in a good stiff breeze. "About Donovan."

"About Donovan? That's funny," Candace said. "I've been thinking about Donovan, too." She still hadn't given him her answer about the Midsummer Dance. She just couldn't decide what to do. On the one hand, he was for sure one of the cutest boys in camp, and she was flattered—beyond flattered—that he'd asked her to the dance. All those girls who liked him, and he'd chosen her—that went to her head like soda bubbles. He loved sailing, like she did, and she thought he was a nice guy.

But Candace took her promises seriously—even her promises to herself. She had really looked forward to a summer without the distraction of boys—and Donovan was very distracting. And she had a feeling that some other girl, like Gaby, maybe, would have more fun at the dance with him than she would.

"What were you thinking?" Valerie asked.

"What was I thinking? What were you thinking? You go first," Candace said.

Valerie neatly cleated the jib line and perched on the starboard side. She was getting to be a pretty good sailor.

"I was thinking that I'm not sure what's holding you back," Valerie said. "From going to the dance with Donovan, I mean. But if it has anything to do with me, don't worry about it. I know you're loyal to your girlfriends, and that's nice. But I'm over Donovan—I never had a serious crush on him in the first place. He's cute and everything, but I'm pulling myself out of the running. Too much competition. And besides, I've got my eye on Zach."

"Zach? Which one is he?"

"You haven't noticed him? He's that tall drink of water on number fourteen over there." She nodded at a lanky redheaded boy expertly maneuvering a Sunfish toward the dock.

"Number fourteen . . ." Candace had seen Zach before, of course, but she'd never noticed him in particular. "Now that you mention it, he is stunning."

"Isn't he?" Valerie said. "If I could just get him to figure out that I'm alive."

"Oh, I think he knows you're alive." Zach tied up his boat and waved at the girls. Valerie waved back. "When we get in, all you have to do is talk to him."

"Right. That's all. Talk to him," Valerie said. "You make it sound so easy, as if you're queen of the flirts. Although you did nab Donovan through some kind of magic alchemy . . ."

"Magic alchemy . . . I'm not sure I believe in

Alyssa and Amy and all that," Candace said. "But she has made some pretty incredible predictions."

"It's a little scary," Valerie said. "That's why I wanted to make sure you knew that if you don't want to go against the Voice of Amy, if you want to say yes to Donovan, you have my blessing. I'm behind you all the way, and I won't even be jealous."

"You won't be jealous? Thanks, Val." Valerie was a great friend, and her gesture was very sweet. But it still didn't solve Candace's problem.

"So have you decided yet?" Valerie asked.

"No," Candace said. "Everyone in the bunk has been bugging me all week."

"We're just curious," Valerie said. "As in dying to know."

"I'm dying to know myself!" Candace said. "It's an impossible choice. On the one hand, a very cute boy likes me. On the other hand, I promised myself no boys. I know some people don't take their promises so seriously, but I'm just not like that. Help me, Valerie. I really don't know what to do!"

"I can't tell you what to do," Valerie said. "You know that. It's your decision in the end. You're the one who has to live with it."

"It's so frustrating," Candace said. "And I'm so tired of worrying about it. This dance is taking up too much space in my brain! Which is exactly why I decided to boycott boys in the first place."

She and Valerie sailed along in silence for a few minutes. Scenes from the first few weeks of camp ran through Candace's mind. There'd been so much talk about magic and fate and coincidence . . .

maybe that was the answer.

"You know what I think I'll do?" Candace said. "I'll let the wind decide for me."

"The wind? What do you mean?"

"I mean, I'll be like Alyssa," Candace said. "I'll let fate, or the universe, or whatever, tell me what to do. It seems to work for her. Look—" She pointed to the mainsail as the wind carried them across the lake. "The wind never steers me wrong. I'll let it decide whether I go to the dance with Donovan or not."

Donovan and Gaby zipped past in their boat, waving. "I'm still not getting you," Valerie said.

"I'll let the regatta decide my fate," Candace said. The big sailing race would take place the next afternoon. "The dance will depend on whether we win or lose the regatta."

"We're going to win that sucker," Valerie said.

"Donovan and Gaby have a chance of beating us," Candace said. "A good chance. Gaby's not nearly as klutzy on the boat as she was at first. Of course, she's not as good a crew as you—" Candace grinned at Val. "But Donovan's great. And he's had a lot of race experience. More than me."

"So what exactly are you going to do?" Valerie said.

It all began to take shape in Candace's mind. Yes. This was the perfect way to make an impossible decision. Leave it to fate. What will be will be.

"If Donovan and Gaby beat us at the regatta, I'll go to the dance with him," Candace said. "But if we beat them, I'll turn him down."

Valerie winced. "That's harsh. If he loses the race,

he loses you too? So he gets to be a two-time loser."

"I don't think he'll be all that upset—about me, I mean," Candace said. "Maybe about the race."

"What if Gaby hears about this?" Valerie said. "She might try to throw the race if she thinks it will get Donovan away from you."

"Throw the race?" Candace hadn't thought of that, and she was genuinely shocked. "Why would anybody try to lose on purpose?"

Valerie laughed. "Candace, think about it. This is Gaby we're talking about. She'll do anything she has to to get what she wants. Throwing a little sailing race is nothing to her."

"Well, she'd better not do that," Candace said. "Donovan will never like her if she does."

"I don't know," Valerie said. "This should be interesting."

"Interesting . . ." Candace said. Valerie had a point. If Gaby knew she could get Donovan by messing up the race, she'd probably do it. And that meant Candace wasn't leaving her decision about the dance up to the wind at all. She'd be leaving it up to Gaby. Not a great idea.

"Let's not tell Gaby," Candace said. "Let's not tell anyone. My little bet with myself will be just between the two of us, okay, Val?"

"Okay," Valerie said. "I won't tell a soul."

"Alyssa, will you bless this for me when I'm done?" Gaby asked, dangling a half-beaded anklet from her finger.

"Will I what?" Alyssa said. "I'm not the Pope, you know."

Gaby and Alyssa sat at a table in arts and crafts, stringing beads. Alyssa was making a necklace to wear to the Midsummer Dance, and Gaby was finishing a good-luck anklet to wear during the sailing race.

"I know you're not the Pope, duh," Gaby said. "But I thought that maybe if you just chant something over it, or say some magic words, or whatever it is you do, it might help me win the race tomorrow."

"I didn't know you cared about winning so much," Alyssa said.

"I care," Gaby said. "But Donovan *really* cares. I was thinking maybe if I help him win, it will make him like me more. We'll share a great memory, of winning the first regatta of the summer together. It can't hurt, right?"

"No, it can't hurt," Alyssa said. "And I'll say any words you want over your anklet, but it won't help. I'm not a wizard."

"You're a psychic," Gaby said. "You can predict what will happen."

"Maybe." Alyssa absentmindedly patted the amethyst in its purse, which hung over the back of her chair. She still hadn't given it back to its rightful owner, whoever she was. Gaby had a feeling Alyssa never *would* give Amy back—at least not until Mandy grabbed her by the ponytail and dragged her to 5C herself.

Gaby grabbed Alyssa's hand. "Please, Alyssa—I can't stand the suspense! Tell me who will win the regatta. You can predict it, I know you can!"

"No," Alyssa said. "Even if I could predict

who'll win, I wouldn't tell you. It might affect your performance."

"No it won't," Gaby said. "I'll try my best no matter what. I promise!"

"But what if I tell you you're going to come in fourth," Alyssa said. "You might get discouraged. Maybe you wouldn't sail your best. I can't be responsible for that."

"Fourth? You think we're going to come in fourth?" Gaby was horrified. If they didn't win, they should at least take second. Donovan was too good to place fourth.

"No, no." Alyssa threaded a large blue bead onto a needle. "That was just an example. I have no idea how you're going to do. But did you see how crazy it made you? That's why I won't tell you my prediction."

"You're no fun," Gaby said.

▲ ▲ ▲

Once Gaby brought up the question of the regatta, Alyssa found herself curious—who *would* win? It seemed to mean an awful lot to both Gaby and Candace.

Gaby finished her anklet, made of blue and green beads. "It's very pretty," Alyssa said. "I like all the watery colors."

"Thank you," Gaby said. "Go ahead, wave your hand over it or something, just for kicks."

"Gaby—" Alyssa felt weird about "blessing" Gaby's anklet when she knew it wouldn't do anything.

"What can it hurt?" Gaby said. "Say something

like, 'I hereby declare that you will win the race.'"

Alyssa waved her hand over the anklet. "May the best sailors win," she said. Gaby frowned. "Sorry," Alyssa added. "That's all I can do."

"Spoilsport." Gaby fastened the anklet around her ankle. "I'll be right back," she said, heading for the bathroom.

While Gaby was in the bathroom, Alyssa slipped Amy out of her purse and, as inconspicuously as possible, cradled the stone in her hand. She closed her eyes and tried to envision the regatta. She pictured the finish line, the boats heading toward it . . . Which boat would cross the line first? She saw two girls, one with a brown ponytail, one with a head full of black braids . . . Candace and Valerie.

Alyssa put the amethyst away. Hmm . . . so Candace and Val would win. Alyssa decided to write the prediction down, for her own satisfaction. Maybe, after the race was over, she'd show it to her bunkmates to impress them even more with her psychic abilities. She grabbed a scrap of paper and wrote, *I, Alyssa, officially predict that the winner of the first regatta will be Candace and Valerie.* Then the bathroom door opened. Alyssa quickly slipped the paper into her purse, next to Amy, before Gaby came back.

▲ ▲ ▲

"Hey, Nat."

Natalie looked up from her *Teen Vogue* to see Logan blocking her sunlight. She was drying her toes in the sun on the dock, where it was quiet now that sailing and canoeing and swimming practices were over for the day. Hank, the sailing instructor, sat outside the boathouse, untangling ropes.

"Hi, Logan." Nat braced herself for more weird behavior. Logan had been nothing but strange since camp had started that summer. Now they were almost a month into it and his behavior had only gotten stranger. Natalie had spent many nights lying in her bunk wondering what was going on with him. Sometimes she felt that he was thinking of her, but then he seemed to avoid her at all costs . . . She couldn't figure it out.

So now, as he stood in her sunlight, she waited to see what he'd do next. Pinch her and run away? Jump into the lake? She was ready for anything except for what he said next.

"Can I sit down?"

"Sure." She slid over a little to make room for him. Now he wanted to sit next to her? She tried to stay cool. "What's up?"

He laughed. "You should see the look on your face."

"What look?" She wasn't aware of a look.

"Like you're afraid I'm going to steal your purse or something," Logan said. "Like I'm crazy."

"I don't think you're crazy," she said.

"Well, I have been acting weird lately, I know that," he said. "But I had a few good reasons."

Natalie hugged one of her knees to her chest. This should be interesting. What would his excuse for his weird behavior be? Possessed by the ghost of a long-dead camper? Afraid he had a special strain of super-contagious yet pox-free chicken pox?

"Well, first, when we got to camp, I wasn't sure how you felt, and that was freaky," Logan said. "I didn't know if you wanted to get back together or not. You never really said, and you were acting kind of nice but not *super* nice, so it was hard to tell."

"I felt the same way about you," Natalie said. "I had no idea whether you still liked me or what."

"I did," he said. "I mean, I do. I missed you a lot when we broke up, but that kind of made me mad. Missing you, you know? I didn't want to miss you, I wanted not to care, but I missed you anyway."

Wow. That was actually kind of sweet, if you chose to read it that way. She decided to say nothing, to wait and see what was coming next.

"I kept hoping that feeling would go away," Logan said. "But it didn't. And then I saw you sailing with Donovan . . . Was that a date, or what?"

"No," Natalie said, and he broke into a relieved grin. "We were just sailing. I figured you wouldn't care. You've barely said two words to me since we got back to camp—till now."

"Yeah, see, I've got a reason for that, too," Logan said. "It's a little strange, though—"

"Strange? I can deal with strange. You should see what's been going on in my bunk this summer."

"Yeah, I saw that stuff in the paper about the big mystery of bunk 6B. What is that about, anyway?"

"I can't tell you right now, and anyway, you're changing the subject."

"Right. I was going to say that I would have tried harder to get back together with you, even after I saw you with Donovan, if it hadn't been for Alaric."

"Who?" The name sounded vaguely familiar.

"Alaric. I'm his CIT. He has an older sister in your bunk. Sloan?"

"Oh, right." Natalie nodded. "What about him?" Logan's explanation was getting odder. What could a ten-year-old boy have to do with her and Logan getting together?

"It sounds kind of stupid, so just listen and don't say anything for a minute, okay?" Logan said.

"Okay."

"You just said something."

Natalie rolled her eyes. She knew when Logan was teasing her. She zipped her mouth closed and raised her eyebrows to make her face say, *Okay now?*

"Okay. Alaric told me that my aura was very green—"

Natalie burst out laughing. "What?!?"

"Nat, you promised."

"Sorry. But come on. Your aura?"

"You're making this pretty hard," Logan said.

Natalie made the zipper motion again.

"Alaric told me that a green aura meant I'd bring trouble to people of the opposite sex," Logan said. "I was a jinx to girls! Of course I didn't take this seriously, even though his mother is a past life regression therapist. I laughed the whole thing off. That's when the bad things started happening."

"What bad things?" Natalie forgot her vow of silence again, but Logan didn't seem to care anymore.

"Remember that little girl at the cookout, the one who burned her tongue on the hot dog?" Logan said. "That was the first sign. I didn't think anything of it, but then that girl at the campfire got stung by some kind of bug. And when I sailed past Donovan and Gaby's boat, Gaby fell overboard. And then you got a splinter in your foot . . . There were other incidents, too, ones you weren't around to see. But they started piling up. And soon I realized that Alaric was right—I really was a jinx to girls."

"Um—okay." What she really wanted to say was, "Who are you and what have you done with Logan?" But she didn't dare, in case it embarrassed him too much to finish the story.

"So that's why I avoided you," Logan said. "I was dying to see you, but whenever I got near you something bad happened, and I didn't want you to get hurt because of me."

"That's so thoughtful," Natalie said, inching away slightly. "But what about now? Here we are, sitting side by side, and nothing bad has happened for five whole minutes."

"Alaric says my aura has blued a little," Logan said. Natalie stifled a laugh. His aura had blued? Words she never thought she'd hear from Logan's mouth—or anybody's. "He's really good at reading auras," Logan said. "Anyway, he says I'm safe now. No more jinx."

"Great!" Natalie said. "So what now?"

"Now," Logan said, "I ask you the big question: Would you like to go to the dance with me? Um, assuming my aura stays clean, of course."

Natalie laughed. The whole camp had magic fever, even cool Logan. And it was so sweet the way he worried about her safety! She didn't hesitate.

"Yes," she said. "I'd love to go to the dance with you."

"Awesome," Logan said.

"It's a trial run," Natalie said. She liked Logan, but she didn't want to rush into anything. She still thought about Reed, the boy from L.A., sometimes. So it was best to take things slow. "After all, you're just recovering from a green aura."

"That's cool," he said. "We're testing the waters. Making sure our auras are a good match."

"Right," she said. But she had a feeling their auras would match up just fine.

▲ ▲ ▲

Alyssa only really knew two girls in 5C—Gwenda and Winnie. And they were both pretty much the last people in camp Alyssa felt like talking to. Gwenda argued with Alyssa every time she opened her mouth. And even though Winnie had publicly apologized for pranking bunk 6B, Alyssa still didn't quite trust her.

But Alyssa couldn't put off returning Amy any longer. Mandy was on her back and her conscience was beginning to bother her. If she'd lost a great amethyst like Amy, she'd want it back, too.

Alyssa got her chance that morning as she passed the newspaper office. She spotted Winnie inside, typing up a sports story. Alyssa just hoped Winnie wouldn't write a *Lakeview Tattler* exclusive on the whole episode.

"Excuse me," Alyssa said. "Did someone in your bunk lose an amethyst?"

Winnie turned around. "Yeah," she said. "We've been wondering what happened to it since the first day of camp."

"Who lost it?" Alyssa asked.

"Do you have it?" Winnie asked.

Alyssa protectively covered the lump in her purse with her hand. She wasn't quite ready to surrender the stone. "Are you the owner?"

"No," Winnie said. "Gwenda is."

Gwenda! Of course. Miss Geology. Spawn of Mr. Spock and a female robot. The least likely person in the whole state of Pennsylvania to believe in Amy's mystical power, who was even more skeptical than Mandy. Alyssa couldn't believe that Gwenda, of all people, was Amy's rightful owner.

"Thank you," Alyssa told Winnie. "I think I know where the amethyst is, and it will be returned to Gwenda very soon."

"Great," Winnie said. "But why don't you just give it back to her now?"

"I have to find the person who has it," Alyssa lied.

"You have it," Winnie said. She pointed to the purse. "Isn't that it? Your hand flew to your purse when I asked you if you had it."

Darn Winnie's reporter's instincts. "No," Alyssa said. "This is . . . well . . . it's just some stuff."

"Whatever." Winnie turned back to her computer and started typing again.

Alyssa left the office. She took Amy out of her pouch and rubbed the shiny purple parts. Poor Amy! To Gwenda rocks were just . . . well, rocks. Amy would get no understanding from someone like that. It was a shame. But Alyssa had to do the right thing.

Right after the big regatta that afternoon.

SIXTEEN

Gaby tied her white sneakers and pulled her hair back into a neat ponytail. Then she double-checked the fastener on her lucky anklet to make sure it was secure. The day of the regatta had come at last, and she was ready to win the battle of the boats.

Most of her bunkmates were out at their various activities, except for Alyssa, who had gotten permission to take a quick shower. Mandy sat on her cot in her little counselor's nook, absorbed in filling out some kind of counselor forms.

As Gaby reached for the sunblock she kept in her cubby, a swatch of familiar fabric caught her eye. A corner of Alyssa's purse—the purse she kept Amy in—peeked out from under the clothes Alyssa had tossed into her own cubby.

Gaby's hand instinctively reached for the purse, but she stopped herself. The day before, in arts and crafts, she thought she'd seen Alyssa slip something into that little purse. What could it have been? Did Alyssa keep anything in there other than Amy? Gaby had never really thought about it before.

Curiosity got the better of her. Gaby decided to take a quick peek inside the purse. She glanced at the bathroom and at Mandy on her bed. No one was looking.

Gaby pulled out the purse and looked inside. Nestled next to the amethyst was a small white piece of paper. She pulled it out and read it.

I, Alyssa, officially predict that the winner of the first regatta will be Candace and Valerie.

Oh, no! Alyssa was predicting her doom!

The water in the shower stopped running. Gaby stuffed the paper inside the purse and put the purse back in the cubby.

"I'm going to the lake now," she said to Mandy.

Mandy looked up from her papers and smiled. "Okay. Good luck, Gaby!"

"Good luck, Gaby!" Alyssa called from the bathroom. "I'll see you down there!"

"Thanks!" Gaby left the bunk and wove her way through the woods to the dock, her mind racing. *We're not going to win? Can it be true? What should I do?*

Should I warn Donovan?

But what good would that do? He'd probably think she was silly for taking her bunkmate's prediction so seriously. He had no idea what kind of strange events had been going on in 6B that summer; he'd never understand. He'd probably be angry with her for having negative thoughts about the race.

When she reached the dock, she found the sailors busy getting their boats ready for the race.

"Hey," Donovan said. "Ready to kick some butt?" He plucked at the worn gold T-shirt he was wearing.

"I'm rocking my lucky T-shirt, so we're good to go."

Gaby smiled wanly at him. So he was superstitious, too. If she brought him bad news, he would probably think of her as a jinx. And what kind of boy would ask a jinx to the Midsummer Dance?

We're going to overcome Alyssa's prediction, Gaby thought. *By sheer force of will. We are going to win this race, and I'll show Donovan what a good sailor I can be.*

She wasn't sure she believed it, but she was ready to try her best.

She lifted her foot to show off her anklet. "I made myself a new good luck charm just for the race."

"Awesome," Donovan said. "Let's hit the water."

His goofy surfer grin melted her heart. Just the sight of him made her completely crumble. *Pull it together,* she told herself. *Concentrate! You're going to win!*

She grabbed a life jacket and they pulled their Sunfish into the water. "I scrubbed the hull this morning," Donovan said. "She's clean and ready to go. Here's our strategy." He put an index finger in his mouth and held it in the air. "The wind is light today, but it could pick up once we're out on the lake. We'll run to the first buoy with the sails let out, and then tighten them up on the second leg and try to pick up speed. Okay?"

"Got it," Gaby said, her mind clicking away with plans. Donovan was in charge of steering the boat and controlling the mainsail. Gaby's job was to work the jib.

The other sailors, including Candace and

Valerie, unfurled their sails and prepared their boats. A good crowd gathered on the dock to watch, including most of bunk 6B. Sloan was cheering for Tom and Alaric. Gaby waved to Alyssa and Natalie, who shouted, "Go, Gaby! Go, Candace! Go, Val!"

Hmph, Gaby thought. She knew who Alyssa secretly favored.

Gaby took her place in the Sunfish. Donovan untied the boat, hopped in, and pushed off from the dock. They sailed out toward the starting line, where Hank sat in a motorboat, ready to start the race.

"Okay, Gaby," Donovan said as they neared the starting point. "It's up to us now. Teamwork. We can do it. Oh, and if I yell at you, don't get upset or take it personally. That's just what happens during races."

Gaby swallowed. So he was going to yell at her even if she did well? No matter what?

"Okay," she said. "I won't."

Hank blew the horn and the race started. Candace and Valerie were first over the starting line, followed by Tom and Alaric. Gaby and Donovan were close behind in third out of ten boats.

"Rats!" Gaby muttered.

"No, we're okay," Donovan said. "Good start. Let out the jib a little."

Gaby let out the smaller front sail. Donovan tilted the tiller to the right and the boat took off. They overtook Tom and Alaric, and were catching up with Candace and Val.

Donovan moved the tiller again, and Gaby instinctively pulled in the jib. "Good," he said. "Here comes the first buoy. Ready about?"

Gaby ducked, and as Donovan shouted, "Hard a-lee," the boom swung around and they turned at the buoy. Gaby popped back up and readjusted her sail. They'd made such a good, tight turn that they'd cut in front of Candace and Val.

"All right!" Donovan said. He tugged on his sail's line, and Gaby tugged on hers. She hardly thought about it; she just did it. They were working in sync, almost as if she knew what he wanted her to do without him having to say it.

Gaby glanced back. The rest of the pack were just rounding the buoy and falling behind fast. Candace pulled up beside Gaby and Donovan. They didn't wave or smile. This was no time to be friendly. This was serious. Gaby could see Candace's determination to win on her face. Donovan's face had the same look.

Their two boats led the pack; the race would come down to them. Only one boat could win. Gaby got caught up in the spirit of competition. She forgot all about Alyssa's prediction. She didn't care what anyone said; she wanted to win.

Candace and Val inched ahead by a nose. Gaby tightened the jib and her boat edged in front. What a cool feeling—she adjusted the sail and the boat responded. She was in control! Well, partly in control. But it was a rush.

"Second buoy!" Donovan called. "Ready about?"

"Hard a-lee!" Gaby shouted, ducking the boom. Another tight turn. They pulled half a length ahead of Candace.

"They need to work on their turns," Donovan shouted, laughing. "We've got them now!"

The wind picked up. Gaby tightened her sail still more. They zipped along, but Candace inched toward them. They were on the last leg now, the crucial part of the race. Gaby glanced back. Logan and Alaric had caught up and were now a boat length behind Candace. The rest of the field was eating their dust, so to speak. Choking on their wake was a better way of putting it, maybe.

They were neck and neck with Candace and Val as they approached the finish line. Gaby read every tiny gesture Donovan made and adjusted her sail accordingly. She leaned forward, willing the boat to go faster. They were going to win—she could feel it.

But just as they crossed the finish line, Candace and Val squeaked ahead. Hank blew the horn. Gaby and Donovan had lost by a nose.

"Shoot!" Donovan stamped his foot. "Shoot shoot shoot!"

Gaby's heart sank. They'd lost. She couldn't believe it. They'd sailed so well; they'd done their best. But Candace and Val had beaten them.

Alyssa was right again.

Logan and Alaric crossed the line third. The other boats wandered in one by one. Donovan steered to the dock and tied up the boat.

The crowd on the dock jumped up and down and cheered. The girls of bunk 6B surrounded Candace and Val, hugging them. Then Alyssa threw her arms around Gaby's neck. Gaby was almost tempted to bow down at Alyssa's feet and say, "I surrender to your power, O

Great One." She might have done it if she hadn't been so mad about losing.

"You were great!" Alyssa said. "You came in second! That's fantastic!"

"I know," Gaby said. "But I wanted to win. We were like a well-oiled machine out there. I really thought we had it. In spite of what *some other people* might have *predicted*."

"It was very close," Alyssa said. "Next time you'll beat them."

"Is that an official prediction?" Gaby said.

Alyssa cast her a wary look, her hand flying to the purse at her side. Gaby wasn't going to admit that she'd peeked in Alyssa's purse, but she couldn't help ribbing her friend a little.

"Woo-hoo!" Candace cheered. She and Val slapped each other five, ten, fifteen, twenty, and then hugged each other in excitement. "That was incredible! We won!"

Gaby was surprised how disappointed she felt. She'd really gotten into the race. For a while there, she wanted to win more than anything. More than *anything*.

Donovan was being a good sport, congratulating the other sailors, but Gaby knew he had to be disappointed. She was, too. Her dreams of the two of them winning together were shot, for now, anyway.

"Good race, Gaby." Candace offered her hand. Gaby shook it. "Second place is no shame. Especially when the finish is so close."

"I know," Gaby said. "But I really wanted to win."

"You never know, Gaby," Candace said.

"Sometimes coming in second has an upside."

She smiled mysteriously, and then disappeared into the crowd.

An upside? What was Candace talking about? What could be good about coming in second?

Still, Gaby latched on to this one small hope. She had no idea what Candace meant, but maybe she was right.

Oh, please let there be an upside, Gaby thought. She prayed to the forces of nature that empowered Alyssa and Amy. *Please, please, an upside . . .*

▲ ▲ ▲

"Nice job." In the boathouse, Donovan offered Candace his hand for a sportsmanlike shake. Candace shook it. "You pulled it out at the very last second."

"It was super close," Candace said. "It could have gone either way."

"But it didn't," Donovan said. "You beat us fair and square. Congratulations! We'll get you next time."

The crowd was beginning to disperse. There was an awkward silence in the boathouse. Candace had been so happy about winning, she'd forgotten for a moment what winning meant. She knew she had something to tell Donovan, but she dreaded saying it.

She pulled off her life jacket and tossed it in the bin. "You sailed a great race out there," she said.

"You did, too," Donovan said. His eyes stayed on her face, bright and expectant. "But the race is over now. Up next—the dance."

Her stomach flipped. "The dance. Right, the dance." Candace swallowed, her mouth dry. "Donovan, you seem really nice and I totally respect you as a sailor. But I'm afraid I can't go to the dance with you, or any boy."

His face fell and he dropped his gaze to the floor. "Oh."

"It has nothing to do with you," Candace said. "If I were going to go with any boy, I'd want to go with you. But I just don't want to do the boy thing this summer. My parents are pressuring me about college already, and I need to concentrate on sailing and summer reading and all that stuff. If I started going out with you, I'd probably fall for you so hard I wouldn't be able to remember my own name."

She smiled at him. She didn't think what she'd just said was true, but she hoped it made him feel better.

He looked up again, smiling ruefully. She could tell he was disappointed. "I thought maybe if you won you'd change your mind," Donovan said.

Actually, it was the other way around, Candace thought, but she didn't let him know how close he'd come to getting a different answer. It might annoy him that she'd left his fate up to a sailing race. But now that it was over, she realized she was glad she'd won the race, and glad she wouldn't be going to the dance with a date. She just didn't feel it.

"I'm sorry, Donovan," she said. "Maybe next year."

"I understand. I actually felt the same way last summer. There was this girl who liked me, but all I wanted to do was sail . . . Anyway, look out. Gaby and I are going to kick your butt next time."

"Kick our butts? Just try it." Candace laughed, relieved to see that he wasn't too heartbroken. "Friends?" she said.

"Friends." He walked out to the dock, leaving her alone in the boathouse.

▲ ▲ ▲

In a show of sportsmanship, Gaby went to the soda machine and bought four celebratory sodas for the two winning boats. When she returned to the boathouse, she found Candace and Valerie standing near the dock. She gave each girl a soda. Donovan sat slouched at the end of the dock, his feet dangling over the water.

"Look at him," Valerie said. "He looks so sad."

"What happened?" Gaby asked.

"Candace told Donovan she couldn't go to the dance with him," Valerie said.

"You did?" Gaby nearly dropped a can of soda on her foot. "Why?"

Candace and Valerie exchanged a glance. "We can tell her," Valerie said. "It's over now."

"Tell me what?" Gaby said.

"I couldn't decide what to do about Donovan," Candace explained. "So I made a kind of deal with myself. If I lost the race, I'd go to the dance with Donovan. But if I won, I wouldn't."

Gaby gasped. "And you won! So you're not going."

Candace nodded. "So he's up for grabs."

So that's what Candace meant by there being an upside, Gaby thought.

"I'm glad we won," Valerie said. "But I do feel sorry for Donovan."

Gaby watched him. He did look sad, and she felt bad for him, too. Not only had he lost the race by a hair, he'd lost his date to the dance. In a way, Gaby thought, the way Candace had handled the whole thing was kind of heartless. Only a girl who wasn't crazy for Donovan could have treated the matter so lightly.

"Do you think I did the wrong thing?" Candace said.

"It wouldn't be fair to go out with him if you're not that into him," Valerie said.

"I guess not," Candace said. "But I feel guilty."

"You'll get over it," Gaby said.

"Gaby," Candace said. "Why don't you go over there and make him feel better?"

"Me?" Gaby said. "How can I make him feel better?"

"You guys have gotten pretty tight since you've been sailing together, haven't you?" Candace said. "Maybe you can commiserate about the race."

"I have an even better idea," Valerie said. "Maybe a date to the dance will cheer him up. Why don't you ask him if he'll be your date, Gaby?"

"Me? Ask him?" Gaby hadn't thought of that. Everyone had been so focused on wondering who *he* would ask, it hadn't occurred to anyone to ask *him.* But it wasn't a bad idea.

"Why not?" Gaby said. They really had grown

closer through sailing. They'd become a team. Gaby looked at him sitting out there on the dock and she realized she no longer thought of him as a boy to be caught like a mouse in a trap. She thought of him as a friend—a friend who happened to be extremely gorgeous.

"Go on." Valerie gave her a little shove. "It can't hurt."

"It's your job as first mate to cheer up a mopey skipper," Candace added. "That's maritime law."

"Okay, but don't watch," Gaby said. "You have to leave, or I'll feel self-conscious."

"All right, all right, just go already," Valerie said, shoving her again.

Gaby walked slowly down the dock. Donovan must have heard her footsteps, but he didn't look up. He just stared at the water under his feet. Gaby sat down next to him.

"Hey," she said.

"Hey." He finally looked up and gave her a halfhearted smile.

"We were great out there," she said. "But Candace and Val are great, too. It's not easy to beat them. But we can, you know. The summer's not over. We'll race them again."

"I know," he said. "You've turned into a pretty good sailor. Remember a few weeks ago, when you first started?"

Gaby laughed. "Remember when I got knocked into the water by the boom?"

"Remember when you capsized about fifty times?"

"How could I forget?" Gaby said. "The sneakers I wore that day are still wet."

"You've gotten a lot better, though," Donovan said. "You respond so fast now. You're really getting the hang of it."

"Thanks," she said. "We're a great team."

"We are, aren't we? Next time, Candace and Val don't have a prayer."

At the mention of Candace's name, he dropped his head and stared at the water again.

"Hey," Gaby said. "I was thinking. I don't have a date to the dance, so . . . I was wondering if you'd go with me."

He looked up, and his face brightened. Gaby took heart. There was hope. He actually seemed interested in her suggestion.

"You know what, matey?" he said. "That's a great idea."

Gaby froze for a second, stunned. *Did he just say yes?*

"That means yes," Donovan added, laughing.

Gaby laughed too. "Great!" Wow. She still could hardly believe it. She asked him, and he said yes. That was easy.

"Are you a good dancer?" she asked.

"Terrible. How about you?"

"Pretty good," Gaby said. "I'll have to teach you."

"Just don't yell at me if I mess up," Donovan said.

"I'll yell at you if I have to," Gaby said. "That's just what happens at dances."

Gaby couldn't wipe the wide smile off her face. She walked back to the bunk to make her huge, major, earthshaking announcement. She did it! She got the guy for once. The perfect, heart-meltingly great guy that she really wanted! And she got him in spite of everything, in spite of all she'd done wrong.

Sometimes fate is on your side, that's all there is to it. Even when it looks as if it isn't.

▲ ▲ ▲

Alyssa was working in the arts and crafts room, making a small box with slots to hold various mystical gems, when Valerie burst in. "Did you hear the incredible, stunning news?" Valerie said. "Donovan is going to the dance with Gaby!"

"Wow," Alyssa said. "How did that happen?"

"Candace turned him down," Valerie said.

"And then Donovan turned around and asked Gaby?" Alyssa found that hard to believe. "That was awful quick."

"She asked him," Valerie said. "And he said yes."

"Good for Gaby," Alyssa said.

Valerie moved aside bottles of glitter and glue and sat down at the table with Alyssa. "You know, Alyssa . . . that means you and Amy were wrong. You predicted Donovan would go to the dance with Candace, not Gaby." She glanced at the purse over Alyssa's shoulder, and Alyssa's face went red. She still hadn't returned Amy to Gwenda, though she planned to do it any minute now. "So maybe Amy's not so powerful after all."

"I know what you're getting at," Alyssa said. "But you're wrong. Technically, Amy was right. If you'll recall, my exact words were, 'Donovan will *ask* Candace to the dance.' That was the way I read the message Amy sent me. And it was correct. Donovan *did* ask Candace. But I never said Candace would say yes. I never said she'd actually *go* to the dance with Donovan."

"But you did advise her to," Valerie said.

"That's different," Alyssa said. "Candace is free to take my advice or reject it."

"I don't know," Valerie said. "That seems like splitting hairs. Isn't it the spirit of the prediction that counts?"

"No," Alyssa said. "When dealing with mystical phenomena, you always have to be careful and precise. Like in those fairy tales where some foolish boy gets three wishes, and the genie grants each wish according to the exact words the boy used when he made the wish, and all the wishes turn out bad?"

"Like when someone wishes to be rich, and the genie makes him rich but he's in jail so he can't enjoy the money?" Valerie said.

"Um, I don't remember that one—"

"Or when a girl wishes to rule the world, so the genie makes all the people in the world disappear so there's nothing in it to rule but plants and rocks?"

"I guess," Alyssa said. She had no idea what Valerie was talking about. "Was that a Twilight Zone?"

"People should always just wish for unlimited wishes," Valerie said. "I don't know why no one ever thinks of that."

"Very true." Alyssa tugged on her purse and

remembered the race prediction she'd made. "Anyway, if you doubt me, look at this." She pulled the slip of paper from her purse and gave it to Valerie.

Valerie read it. "You predicted that we would win the race? When did you write this?"

"Yesterday," Alyssa said.

"You could have written this prediction five minutes ago," Valerie said.

"But I didn't," Alyssa said. "I wrote it yesterday. I swear. I superswear."

"I believe you," Valerie said. "I know how seriously you take your superswears."

Alyssa patted the amethyst in her purse. "I'm going to miss this little rock."

Valerie frowned in sympathy. "We all will."

Alyssa stopped at the threshold of the nature shack and peered into the room. Sitting quietly at a table with her back to the door was Gwenda. She appeared to be working intently on a special project. *Probably building a robot to help her take over the world*, Alyssa thought.

Okay, not fair. Alyssa patted Amy nervously. Gwenda wasn't really so bad. And after all, she was going to be Amy's new Keeper. Her new home. Alyssa sighed. She was going to miss feeling the weight of the stone in her hand. But it was time to face the music.

Alyssa stepped into the shack and cleared her throat. "Gwenda? Hi."

Gwenda turned around and smiled at her. "Hi, Alyssa. Here to work on your project for the nature fair?" On the table in front of her was a display case for her collection of rocks and minerals, with labels and detailed descriptions of their properties.

"Uh, no," Alyssa said. "I have something to give you. Or rather, to return to you." She took off her purse and held it out for Gwenda, who opened it and looked inside.

"My amethyst! Where did you find it?"

"On the ground near the camp entrance," Alyssa said. "On the very first day of camp."

"I've been looking for it everywhere," Gwenda said. Alyssa flinched at hearing Gwenda refer to Amy as "it." She was so used to thinking of the amethyst as "she." Maybe that was a little nutty.

Gwenda took the amethyst out of the purse and held it in her hand, jumping just a little with excitement. "I'm so glad you found it! Thank you so much for returning it to me. It's a great specimen, isn't it?"

Gwenda held the amethyst in the light. The purple parts sparkled.

"Yes," Alyssa said sadly. "It's a great specimen."

"I'm so psyched to have it back!" Gwenda said. "I need it for my nature project. See?"

Gwenda showed Alyssa the display box she was making. At the top was a label reading THE QUARTZ RAINBOW. Inside each small section nestled a different variety of quartz, arranged by color from lightest (rock crystal) to darkest (black onyx). The box labeled AMETHYST was empty.

Two very different girls making two oddly similar boxes. What was that about?

"I started planning this project before I even left for camp," Gwenda said. "But it's incomplete without an amethyst. I need a purple stone or the rainbow idea doesn't work at all. And they're hardly indigenous to this region."

"Right." All the quartzes were so beautiful,

from smoky to rose to citrine. But Amy was the most beautiful of all.

"I was afraid my project was ruined," Gwenda said. "I tried to remake my quartz display box so Roseanne wouldn't realize that the purple rock was missing. But anyone who knows minerals would notice the omission."

"That's all the amethyst is to you—a purple rock?" Alyssa said.

"Of course not," Gwenda said. "An amethyst is a macrocrystalline quartz, a low-temperature stable form of silicon dioxide. The purple color comes from the presence of iron during formation."

"That's heartwarming," Alyssa said.

Gwenda gave her a funny look, and Alyssa immediately felt bad for making a snarky comment. She'd obviously touched a nerve.

"You know what?" Gwenda said. "To me, science *is* heartwarming. I know some people don't get it, but I love science, and I think it's beautiful."

"You're right," Alyssa said. "I'm sorry. A lot of people don't get the stuff I'm into, either."

"What are you doing for your nature fair project?" Gwenda asked.

"I don't know yet," Alyssa said. "I still have to figure a few things out."

"Well, thanks for returning my amethyst to me," Gwenda said. "You saved my project." She put Amy into her slot in the box of quartz minerals. Now the collection was complete.

"You're welcome," Alyssa said.

Alyssa knew she'd done the right thing. Still,

leaving the nature shack and heading for dinner, she felt as if a part of her was missing. Maybe it was *just* Amy, but Alyssa was afraid it could be her psychic gift as well.

▲ ▲ ▲

"Are you okay?" Gaby asked Alyssa as she sat down at bunk 6B's table in the mess hall that evening.

"Yeah, you look like your dog just died," Chelsea said.

"Hey," Natalie said. "Don't say that. I'm touchy on that subject."

"I thought Tumtum was okay," Gaby said.

"He is okay," Natalie said. "And I want him to stay that way. No jinxing."

"Jinxing?" Chelsea rolled her eyes. "I can't say anything around here. You've heard of political correctness? Well, this bunk is cursed by mystical correctness. Nobody can make a move for fear of bringing on bad luck."

"We don't have to worry about that anymore," Alyssa said. "Amy is gone. Back to her original owner, Gwenda of bunk 5C."

"Let's all bow our heads for a moment of silence," Sloan said.

Everyone at the table bowed their heads. Well, almost everyone.

"Oh, please," Mandy snapped. "It was a rock!"

"A mineral, actually," Alyssa said. "Quartz, to be exact. Silicon dioxide."

"You can always buy another amethyst when you get home from camp," Natalie said.

"I know," Alyssa said. "But there will never be one

like Amy." She sighed. "It's a shame. Gwenda doesn't know what she has. She'll never connect with Amy the way I have. There's about as much chance of that as there is of snow in July."

A few of the girls laughed. "Snow in July," Candace said. "Now that would be *really* weird."

"If you can make it snow in July," Mandy said, "*then* I'll believe in magic."

"It's a deal," Alyssa said.

"You're not really saying it's going to snow, are you?" Brynn said.

Alyssa shrugged and smiled mysteriously. Of course it wouldn't snow. But now that the words were out of her mouth, she couldn't take them back. "Who knows?" she said. "Anything could happen."

Brynn sat on a stone bench near the campfire that night, waiting for her bunkmates to join her. Instead, Jordan plopped down beside her.

"Hey," she said.

"Hey," he said. "Listen—I wanted to apologize to you about Winnie. I know she apologized in the paper, but I wasn't sure what you were thinking. I mean, she and I were working on a story together when she invaded your bunk's privacy, and I wanted to make sure you knew I had nothing to do with it. I'd never tell a reporter to prank somebody or go through someone's personal stuff—"

"I know that," Brynn said. "Don't worry, Jordan. I don't blame you for any of that. Anyway, it's over now."

"Phew. Good. I'm glad you're not mad at me."

"I'm totally not."

"You did some great investigative work," Jordan said. "Figuring out what Winnie was up to and everything."

"Well—" Brynn hated to admit how she found out who'd pranked them—sneaking into 5C wasn't exactly a sterling example of journalistic ethics. "Gaby should get most of the credit for that."

"It was you, too," Jordan said. "Anyway, I thought it was cool."

"Thanks."

"So, you going to the dance tomorrow night?"

"I was planning on it. Isn't everyone?"

"I guess so," Jordan said. "Are you going with anyone?"

"Just my buds."

"Oh." He paused. She could hear him swallowing his nervousness even over the crackling of the fire. "I know this is kind of last minute, but would you like to go to the dance with me?"

This sudden thrill made her suck in her breath. Did this mean what she hoped it meant—that he wanted to get back together, too?

"I'd love to," she said.

"Excellent," Jordan said. "I—I've been hoping we could get back together this summer. I just wasn't sure what you were thinking."

"I was hoping that, too," Brynn said. "But I thought you didn't want to. You didn't seem that interested at first."

"Well . . . I was trying to play it cool," Jordan said.

"And, you know, last spring I kind of got the feeling you might not want to hang out. I think your exact words were 'It's over.'"

Brynn laughed. "Those were not my exact words. I just couldn't juggle rehearsing a play and having a boyfriend. It wasn't fair to either one of us. But once I got to camp I was doing the same thing as you—playing it cool."

"I guess the playing it cool method doesn't work too well when both people do it," Jordan said.

"Guess not."

"But—you *do* want to get back together?" Jordan asked.

"Yeah. I do," Brynn said.

"All right!" Jordan said. "Well, I'll let you sit with your friends. See you tomorrow night. If not before."

"Okay."

Brynn's face flushed with happiness. She felt so warm, she had to turn away from the fire.

"What happened?" Natalie asked. She and Candace rushed over to Brynn and sat down in the spot Jordan had left empty. "We saw you talking to Jordan and were afraid to come over in case we were interrupting something."

"Jordan wants to get back together!" Brynn said. "And he asked me to the dance."

Natalie and Candace squealed and hugged Brynn. "That's fantastic!" Candace said. "You guys belong together."

"We'll have the best time tomorrow night," Natalie said. "Even if we do have to wear our bathing suits."

EIGHTEEN

"It's kind of chilly for bathing suits, don't you think?"

Gaby buttoned her pink sleeveless dress over her red one-piece swimsuit. The girls in bunk 6B were getting ready for the Midsummer Dance together. A cool breeze blew in through the window. Gaby shivered.

"I think the breeze is refreshing," Valerie said. "After all the hot weather we've had."

"Still," Natalie said as she zipped up her white eyelet dress. "If we have to dance in our swimsuits, it would be nice not to freeze."

"My bikini is ruining the lines of my dress," Chelsea complained. The straps of her yellow bikini halter showed under her blue spaghetti-strap dress. "This is so not fair."

"It's only one dance," Alex said. "We'll ask the DJ to play a really short song."

"Then we'll pull off our dresses, dance around in our suits, and put our dresses back on as soon as the song ends," Candace said.

"It's going to be mortifying," Gaby said.

"It will be over like *that*." Mandy snapped her fingers. In solidarity with her campers, she was wearing a bathing suit under her denim skirt and polo shirt.

"Don't you have something a little dressier to wear, Mandy?" Chelsea asked. The sixth division traditionally wore fairly fancy dresses to the Midsummer Dance.

"These are the fanciest clothes I've got," Mandy said with a grin. "Don't worry—I'll pick some honeysuckle to wear in my buttonhole and I'll be fine."

"Here, take one of mine." Alyssa wore the necklace she'd made in arts and crafts and a wildflower wreath in her hair. She plucked off one of the wildflowers and gave it to Mandy, who threaded it through the buttonhole on her polo.

"Thanks," Mandy said.

Gaby checked herself out in the mirror. She wanted to look perfect for Donovan. But something was missing.

Alyssa seemed to read her mind. She offered Gaby a pretty blue flower from her wreath. "You take one, too, Gaby. Tonight's the big night!"

"Thanks, Alyssa." Gaby pinned the flower in her hair with a barrette.

"Hello? Anyone home?" There was a knock at the cabin's screen door. Gaby froze.

"It's Donovan!" Brynn whispered. "Gaby, are you ready?"

"I don't know. Inspection!" Gaby twirled in front of her bunkmates. "Do I look ready?"

"You look great, Gaby," Alyssa said.

"You look perfect," Natalie said.

"Perfect," Candace said. "And beautiful."

"Okay," Gaby said. "Here I go."

"We'll be right behind you," Mandy said.

Gaby went outside to meet Donovan. He looked more adorable than ever. A month of camp sunshine had reddened his cheeks and nose and put a bit of gold in his hair, making him glow. He wore a navy jacket over a blue Oxford button-down shirt and neat cotton pants cinched with a canvas belt showing different nautical flags. He looked every inch the preppy sailor boy, and at that moment Gaby thought a preppy sailor boy was the highest life-form in the universe.

"Hey, there, skipper," she said.

"Ahoy there, first mate," he said. "Shall we shove off?"

He took her arm and walked her up the path toward the main lodge. The dance was held on the porch and the front lawn. Gaby thought Camp Lakeview had never looked so beautiful. The sun was setting over the lake, the fireflies beginning to haunt the trees. Up ahead the music grew louder, and soon they were there, at the dance.

Glowing Japanese lanterns blew in the chilly breeze, casting a romantic light on everyone. If she squinted, Gaby could make the crowd of gawky, sun-burned campers look like graceful, romantic couples. *If* she squinted. Hard.

DJ Hank, the sailing instructor, played dance music at the turntable. Mandy reported for duty at the refreshment stand, offering punch and soda and snacks. Everything was trimmed in honeysuckle and roses.

The wind picked up a bit, and clouds passed over the sun. The lightning bugs disappeared, as if they were hibernating.

"Chilly?" Donovan asked Gaby.

Gaby nodded. "It's getting weirdly cold, don't you think?"

"Want to borrow my jacket?" Donovan said.

"Maybe later," Gaby said. "Want to dance? That's a good way to warm up."

"Okay," Donovan said. "As long as you don't make fun of me."

"I won't. Do you know how to Pogo?" Gaby hopped up and down as if jumping on a pogo stick. "It's pretty much the easiest dance ever invented."

Donovan hopped up and down with Gaby. The rest of her bunk had arrived, and they crowded onto the dance floor. Brynn danced with Jordan, Natalie with Logan, Alex with Adam, Jenna with David. Alyssa and a bunch of other girls pogo'd together in a clump. Gaby took both of Donovan's hands. He was doing great. "See?" she shouted over the music. "It's not hard."

Donovan grinned his charming grin. His hair bounced up and down as he danced. They pogo'd to every song, even the slow ones, until they were dying of thirst and could pogo no more.

"Let's get something to drink," Gaby said.

They dodged the younger kids, boys and girls chasing one another around, on their way to the refreshment table.

"Looks like you're having fun out there," Mandy said, pouring Gaby some punch.

"We are," Gaby said.

Another chilly gust blew, and Mandy said, "We should be serving hot apple cider instead of punch."

Winnie and another 5C girl stopped by for a drink. "Hey, Gaby," Winnie said. "Hope you've got your bathing suit on under that dress."

"Yeah," said the other girl. "Get ready, because we're not letting you off the hook."

"We're ready," Gaby said. "Don't worry."

"What's that all about?" Donovan asked.

"This stupid bet we made," Gaby said. "Long story."

"Oh, right. The bathing suits," Donovan said. "Want to sit down for a minute?" He led Gaby to the edge of the dance floor. She thought they'd sit in the chairs that lined the side, but he kept going, underneath the Japanese lanterns, across the path, and into the woods. "Here," he said. They sat under a big old elm tree. Gaby leaned against its thick trunk and sipped her punch.

"You've got the pogo down," Gaby said.

"Thanks," Donovan said. "My other dance moves could use some practice."

"I'll be glad to practice with you, if you want," Gaby said. "Any time."

They sat quietly for a few minutes, sipping their drinks and listening to their friends laughing and cheering across the path. Gaby tried to think of something to say.

"I could use some extra practice, too," she said. "In sailing, I mean."

"No problem," Donovan said. "Why don't we

spend a few of our free periods sailing together? By the end of the summer you'll be an old salt."

"Excellent." Gaby felt her face glow. Extra sailing practice with Donovan! This summer was about to get a whole lot better.

The sun had set, and the night got downright cold. Gaby rubbed her arms.

"Here," Donovan said. He took off his jacket and draped it over Gaby's shoulders.

"Thank you," Gaby said. He was such a gentleman. She looked at his face in the moonlight. He was grinning his wide, goofy grin. Suddenly Gaby had a vision—of herself kissing him.

Donovan must have read her mind. He leaned forward and kissed her right on the lips.

"Wow," Gaby said.

"Yeah," Donovan said. "You know what? That's something else we ought to practice more."

"You're already pretty good at it," Gaby said.

"So are you," Donovan said. "But a little practice won't hurt, right?"

"Right," Gaby said. She kissed him again. *After all*, she thought, *practice makes perfect.*

Alyssa was so busy dancing, she hardly noticed how cold the night had gotten. But later in the evening she realized a lot of the campers were wearing sweaters and sweatshirts over their fancy dance clothes.

"I wish I'd brought a shawl," Natalie said. "Look—I've got goose bumps!"

"Me too," Alyssa said.

"Okay, kids," DJ Hank stopped the music and took the microphone. "Hope you're all having a good time. Are you?"

"Yeah!" The whole camp cheered.

"All right," Hank said. "I've got a special announcement to make. The girls of bunk 5C inform me that the girls of 6B have to make good on a little wager they made. Can I get all the 6B girls on the dance floor?"

"Oh, no," Alyssa said. "Here we go."

Mandy herded all her girls to the middle of the dance floor. Alyssa saw Gaby sitting off to the side with Donovan and waved her over.

"Get over here, Gaby!" Alyssa called. "You're not weaseling out of this!"

Gaby laughed as Donovan pushed her onto the dance floor with the others.

"I can't believe we have to do this in front of the whole camp!" Chelsea said.

"Come on—it'll be fun!" Brynn said. "A Lakeview experience you'll never forget."

"That's for sure," Jenna said with a laugh.

"All right, girls," Hank said. "Time to dance in your bathing suits. Let's boogie!"

Alyssa and her bunkmates pulled their dresses over their heads and huddled together on the dance floor in their bathing suits. The crowd laughed and clapped.

"Brrr!" Tori said. "It's freezing!"

"Start dancing!" Mandy said. "It will warm us up!"

Might as well enjoy it, Alyssa thought. She and her friends started dancing, and soon they didn't feel cold at all. They formed a kick line, which was greeted with wild applause. They sang along to the song Hank played.

"This is fantastic!" Natalie cried.

"So much fun!" Candace shouted.

Suddenly, Alyssa felt something cold and wet land on her shoulder. She ignored it, but it happened again. And again. Finally, she looked up. And she couldn't believe what she saw.

Big, fat, beautiful white flakes were floating down from the sky.

A flake landed on Alyssa's forearm. She touched it. Cold, wet, white . . . It was snow!

Snow! In July!

Squeals of delight rang out over the camp.

"It's snowing!" Brynn cried.

"I don't believe it!" Mandy said.

"Ladies and gentlemen, I do believe it's snowing!" Hank said. "Time for some new music." He pressed some buttons on his iPod and soon the song "Let It Snow" poured out of the speakers.

"Let it snow!" Brynn sang out. The rest of the campers swarmed the dance floor to dance in the snow. Alyssa watched the scene in amazement. Donovan took Gaby's hands and swung her around. Natalie and Logan kissed under the falling flakes. Brynn snuggled with Jordan, and Alex with Adam. Jenna and David tried to catch snowflakes on their tongues.

"Isn't it romantic?" Valerie said. She took Alyssa's hand. Soon they were joined by Candace, Priya, Chelsea, Tori, Sloan, and Mandy. They danced in a circle, holding hands. The rest of their bunkmates joined the circle and they spun around on the dance floor, shouting, "Let it snow!"

The 5C girls clapped and laughed and danced around them. "You girls sure know how to pay off a bet in style!" Winnie said.

"Alyssa predicted it!" Brynn shouted. Alyssa moved to stop her, then decided against it. The amethyst was back with Gwenda. It wasn't a secret anymore, so there was no need to keep quiet about it.

"That's right!" Candace said. "Alyssa—you predicted this! You predicted snow in July—and here it is!"

"It's a miracle!" Priya said.

"This is so weird," Valerie said.

"But lovely!" Natalie said.

Even Chelsea was impressed. "Wow," she kept saying over and over, as if she were in some kind of trance. "Wow. Snow. Wow. I don't believe it. Snow. Wow."

Alyssa didn't know what to say. Was it magic? Did she really have the power to predict the weather?

"Mandy," Sloan said. "You said that if it snowed in July, you'd believe in magic."

All eyes were on Mandy. Would she admit that she believed in magic?

"Well, we've had some pretty weird weather patterns this year," Mandy said. "Remember that seventy degree day back in February? And we *are* in the mountains—"

"Mandy, come on," Sloan said. "Alyssa mentioned snow last night at dinner—and here it is!"

"When is the last time you saw snow here at camp?" Jenna said.

"Okay, you're right," Mandy said. "It's an amazing coincidence."

"A coincidence?" Gaby said.

"It's strange, okay?" Mandy said. "I admit it. This is very strange. Mysterious. Baffling. A miracle! I believe! I believe in magic!"

"Hurray!" her campers shouted, laughing. "Mandy believes in magic!"

They danced some more as the snow poured down. Soon everything around them—the grass, the trees, the paths and the picnic tables—all were covered with a thin coat of white.

"It's so beautiful!" Natalie said.

"It's like dancing in a fairyland," Alyssa said.

Whap! Something cold and wet splattered against Alyssa's back. Alyssa whipped around. Logan, Jordan, and Donovan approached the dance floor packing snowballs in their hands.

"Snowball fight!" Brynn cried, swiping a handful of snow and packing it into a snowball as well as she could. "Fire!"

The boys tossed snowballs at them. The girls fired back. A few of the little kids built tiny snowmen on the grass. Alyssa stuck out her tongue to catch a fat snowflake. The whole camp was giddy as everyone played in the summer snow.

"This must be the strangest Midsummer Dance in the history of camp," Valerie said. "Girls dancing in the snow in their bathing suits! It's wild!"

"Maybe so," Alyssa said, "but isn't it great?"

Everyone agreed that it was.

chapter

NINETEEN

"I can't believe I have to go swimming now," Gaby said the next morning. "I mean, it snowed last night! These are, like, polar bear conditions."

But the sun was strong, the snow had melted, and the day was warming up. Summer had returned. Last night's snow felt like a dream.

"Did it really snow?" Alyssa said.

"It really snowed," Natalie said in a stunned voice. "It really snowed."

"It hardly feels real," Gaby said.

"Magic never does," Sloan said.

"That's okay," Gaby said. "There's more magic to come. Camp is only half over!"

▲ ▲ ▲

"Alyssa, can I talk to you a minute?"

Alyssa was surprised to see Gwenda at the softball field. Just the sight of Gwenda gave Alyssa a pang—*Amy*. Alyssa missed her.

"Sure," Alyssa said. "What's up?" It was a

beautiful day and she was macrame-ing a plant holder while watching Alex, Valerie, Priya, and Jenna play softball. Alyssa felt a little sleepy that morning. The night before, at the Midsummer Dance, she and her friends had danced together in the snow until midnight, when Mandy had to drag them back to their bunk.

Gwenda sat down on the grass and watched the softball game. She looked uncomfortable. But then, she usually did. She wasn't what Alyssa would call a social person.

Alyssa waited for Gwenda to say whatever was on her mind, but she didn't. *Guess it's up to me to get things started*, Alyssa thought.

"Did you have a good time at the dance last night?" she asked Gwenda.

Gwenda nodded. "The snow was beautiful. But highly unlikely this time of year. It came out of nowhere, a total shock. It didn't even show up on my weekly meteorology report."

Meteorology report? "Snow in July is definitely strange," Alyssa said. "But that just made it seem even cooler." After another awkward silence, she added, "So—you said you wanted to talk to me?"

"I heard what you did with the amethyst," Gwenda said.

Alyssa froze. What she did with the amethyst? Had she done something wrong? Had she damaged it in some way?

Gwenda must have read the panic on Alyssa's face, because she said, "No, it's okay. I don't mean that you did something bad. I'm talking about the predictions. Interpreting dreams. I heard some of your bunkmates talking about it last night. They said you even predicted the snow."

"It's true," Alyssa said. "That amethyst is magical."

"I don't believe in magic," Gwenda said. "And I doubt your predictions had anything to do with magic. The evidence is circumstantial and highly suspect. Yet still strangely compelling. So compelling that I set up an experiment. I tried to make some predictions myself, using the amethyst."

"You did?" Alyssa was amazed. "What happened?"

"Well, this morning I tried interpreting some dreams. Winnie dreamed that she was eating a hamburger at a picnic table and a squirrel kept taking bites out of it. Weird, huh? So I concentrated and thought about what it could mean. I told her the squirrel represented time, taking bites out of her life."

"That's depressing," Alyssa said. "And kind of gross."

"Time is going by quickly," Gwenda said. "I'll be in eighth grade next year."

"Yeah, but that's not exactly Death's door. What did Winnie say about your interpretation?"

"She said the squirrel was definitely biting a hamburger, not time, and mostly she was mad at the squirrel because she was hungry and wanted to eat the burger herself," Gwenda said. "Then she told me to give up."

Alyssa shook her head. "There's an art to this,

Gwenda. You can't just blurt out any old thing. People take their dreams seriously."

"I know. The truth is, when she told me her dream, I didn't see anything. No visions or flashes of understanding. I just made something up."

"Were you holding Amy while you interpreted the dream?"

"Amy?"

"I named your amethyst Amy."

"Oh. Yes, I was holding it. I tried a couple more times, but nothing came to me. Nothing at all. I guessed that we'd have oatmeal for breakfast, but we had bacon and eggs. I felt like a fake." She paused, picking at the grass. "How do you do it, Alyssa? How do you see the future? How do you make accurate predictions? Where do your visions come from?"

"I—I don't know. I guess I've got a gift," Alyssa said, hoping she sounded more modest than she felt. She did have a gift—she knew she did. Maybe it had something to do with the amethyst; maybe it didn't. The point was, Alyssa could read people, and she could read the world around her. The signs, the symbols, the portents. She was good at it.

"Well, whatever it is, I don't have it," Gwenda said.

"I still don't see why you're fessing up to me," Alyssa said.

"It's by way of explanation for what I'm about to do," Gwenda said. "Which, without the explanation, might appear illogical."

"Feel free to be illogical around me," Alyssa said. "I don't mind."

Gwenda reached into her pocket and pulled out the amethyst. She offered it to Alyssa.

"Would you like to have it back?" she said.

Alyssa gasped. There she was, good old Amy, sparkling purply in the sun. Alyssa had missed her so much! She reached for the rock, picked it up, and wrapped her fingers around it. It seemed to warm at her touch. Alyssa grinned broadly. "Thank you, Gwenda!"

"I still need it for the nature fair," Gwenda said. "So don't lose it. But after that, you can keep it for good. I can always get another amethyst for my collection. But you seem to have a strong connection to this one. It wouldn't make sense for me to keep it when you can do so much more with it. To me, *science* is magic. I don't understand all that psychic stuff. But if it works, it works."

"Gwenda, you're the sweetest!" Alyssa threw her arms around Gwenda's neck in a big hug.

"Thanks," Gwenda said. "You *will* let me display the stone at the fair, right?"

"Of course, of course." Alyssa was so thrilled to have Amy again. She squeezed Amy tight and vowed never to let her go.

▲ ▲ ▲

"Alyssa, what are we having for dinner tonight?" Brynn asked. "I'm hungry now, but I don't want to spoil my appetite by eating all these chips if we're having something good."

"Just a minute, I'll check." Alyssa grabbed Amy from under her pillow and rubbed the smooth purple facets. She closed her eyes and concentrated. Suddenly, she thought she smelled fried chicken.

There was her answer.

"Fried chicken," she said, opening her eyes.

Brynn ate a chip, and then rolled the bag closed. "Excellent. I'll save room for fried chicken."

"It's so nice to have Amy back," Natalie said. "It makes planning the future so much easier."

Chelsea rolled her eyes. "I'll never believe Alyssa is psychic, period."

"What if we get to the mess hall and we're having fried chicken?" Gaby said. "Then will you believe?"

"No," Chelsea said. "I said never, and I mean never."

"Dinnertime, girls," Mandy said. "Let's go get some fried chicken."

"So you believe in the amethyst's power now, Mandy?" Alyssa said.

"Sure," Mandy said. "It was the snow that got me. That was too weird to be believed."

Alyssa put Amy in her little purse, ready to go to dinner. She didn't care whether Chelsea believed—Amy was good luck and that's all there was to it.

The bunk 6B girls walked together to the mess hall and took their table. "It does smell like chicken," Candace said.

"Please," Alyssa said. "Why do you doubt? Amy is infallible."

A CIT brought a platter of food and set it on the table. Alyssa stared at it.

"What's that?" she asked.

"Chicken cacciatore," the CIT said.

"See," Chelsea said. "That's not fried chicken. Alyssa the Infallible is wrong again."

"No I'm not." Alyssa took some vegetables from the platter. "I said chicken, and this is chicken. Amy and I are still right."

"You said *fried* chicken," Alex said. "This is chicken cacciatore. That's totally different."

"No it's not. It'd be one thing if I had said meat loaf and they brought chicken. But I said chicken and that's what they brought." So her prediction was a little off; there was no way Alyssa was admitting it to Chelsea.

"Maybe you don't get the difference because you're a vegetarian," Chelsea said. "But trust me, if I ordered fried chicken in a restaurant and they gave me this, I'd send it back."

"Quit picking on Alyssa," Gaby said. "Chicken cacciatore is close enough."

"Girls, girls!" Mandy said. "Let's agree to disagree and start eating."

"We'll never all agree," Candace said. "That's the fun of it."

Alyssa patted Amy in her purse. Fried chicken, cacciatore, it didn't really matter. Deep in her heart, Alyssa didn't really know if the amethyst brought her magic. But it was so much fun to believe she did. Just thinking about magic seemed to make it happen—like snow in July.

She saw a vision, clear as a movie, of a long string of happy days stretching through the summer. Camp was half over, but Alyssa knew the best was still to come.

Get out your hankies ...

Camp Confidential
is coming to an end.
Be sure not to miss the
heartbreaking final book,
Suddenly Last Summer,
in bookstores this summer.